"I didn't finish my apology..."

Scott turned the small wineglass between his thumb and forefinger, staring into the liquid. "What I said about your wanting to be kissed...."

Andy stiffened. "It's all right, Scott. No apology is necessary."

"You're wrong," he said softly. "It was far from all right and I sincerely apologize." He placed his wineglass on the table near her and slid from the couch onto the floor by the hassock where she sat.

"I'm apologizing because I may need to do it again after this." He reached over, pulling her to the floor with him. Andy could have stopped him, but she didn't. She could have moved away, but she didn't. Instead she allowed him to push her backward onto the plush carpet. Not only that, but she pulled him down with her, impatient to feel his mouth on hers again....

ABOUT THE AUTHOR

Zelma Orr had a most interesting career before turning to writing full-time: she was a U.S. Customs Officer for the Treasury Department in her home state of Texas. Zelma loves to travel and keeps a diary of the places she has visited to use for story ideas in future books.

Books by Zelma Orr

HARLEQUIN AMERICAN ROMANCE

HARLEQUIN INTRIGUE

These books may be available at your local bookseller.

Don't miss any of our special offers. Write to us at the following address for information on our newest releases.

Harlequin Reader Service
P.O. Box 52040, Phoenix, AZ 85072-2040
Canadian address: P.O. Box 2800, Postal Station A,
5170 Yonge St., Willowdale, Ont. M2N 6J3

Someone Else's Heart

ZELMA ORR

Harlequin Books

TORONTO • NEW YORK • LONDON
AMSTERDAM • PARIS • SYDNEY • HAMBURG
STOCKHOLM • ATHENS • TOKYO • MILAN

Published March 1985

First printing January 1985

ISBN 0-373-16094-1

Chapter One

"Andy!"

"Yo?" The voice from beneath the plane was muffled, as though the speaker had a mouth full of cotton.

As a matter of fact, it was a mouth full of rubber gaskets that wouldn't benefit from being placed on the oily surface beneath the plane.

"Mr. Rawlins is here to talk to you about that trip you scheduled for Monday."

"Be right there," the muffled voice promised. A moment later, orange-clad legs appeared, followed by the balance of a figure outfitted in bright coveralls. Giving the roller platform a shove, Andy turned toward the voice, waving to indicate having heard what Jere said.

Long legs made quick work of the distance between the plane being serviced and the door where Jere stood talking to a man dressed in a dark business suit.

Reaching the doorway and pulling the mechanic's cap from her head, she shook out her short, blond-streaked hair and grinned at her brother.

"It's ready to go, Jere," she told him, turning

apologetically to look at the man beside him. "Give me a moment to wash my hands, Mr. Rawlins, and I'll be with you."

He wasn't much taller than she was, maybe three or four inches, which still made him tall, since she stood five feet ten inches in stocking feet. His hair was the color of dull silver with the hint of the darker color it must have been at one time. The sheen suggested a recent shampoo, and the style emphasized its thickness.

The odd shade of hair accentuated eyes the color of the Colorado sky after a rain, framed by charcoal lashes. The electric-blue eyes narrowed as they went over the woman in front of him.

"There must be some mistake," the quiet voice said. "I was scheduled to fly with Andy Timmons, not a woman."

"You have something against female pilots, Mr. Rawlins?" she asked pleasantly.

The expression in her voice made him stiffen, because her eyes had not changed and she was smiling.

"I prefer a male pilot. No offense, Miss...uh... Andy," he said.

"Timmons, Mr. Rawlins. Andy Timmons," she supplied graciously.

He looked her up and down, taking in the wide mouth, the tip of her tongue caught between the edge of her teeth as she continued to smile at him, the dark-blond hair and the wide gray eyes that had a tendency to narrow against the bright sunlight. She stood with her legs slightly bent at the knees.

Mr. Rawlins turned toward Jere. "If it can possibly

be arranged, I'd like to have you pilot the plane, Mr. Timmons. If need be, I can change the flight from Monday to another day later in the week."

Andy glanced over the potential customer as he talked. She liked what she saw. Robustly built, he probably lifted weights, she decided. The suit he wore was specially tailored to fit the width of his shoulders; it was a dark-gray material, contrasting sharply with his bright eyes and silver hair.

She so seldom saw suits such as Mr. Rawlins wore that it was a pleasant surprise to see how nice it looked. Jere and her father, Avery Timmons, wore coveralls, much the same as she did. So did the other mechanics around the field and the pilots that flew in from time to time.

Jere looked at her a moment before he turned back to the other man. "My dad won't be available next week, Mr. Rawlins, but—"

The man made an impatient gesture with his hand and Andy's eyes followed the movement of long fingers. "How about you, then? Surely, your wife can manage here a few days while you're away."

Jere shot a look at Andy, grinning at the reference.

Andy's gaze didn't waver as she said, "Of course, Jere, you can do it. Just remember to put plenty of barf bags in the cockpit and take an extra box of Dramamine with you. I'll try not to foul up the books while you're gone, but I don't guarantee you anything. The De Havilland Otter has been serviced for the trip. I'll give you some instructions on how to start it and take off and land before you leave Monday."

With a last friendly smile at Mr. Rawlins, she

turned and made her way through the next room out onto the field adjacent to the building. She felt the daggers in the look Mr. Rawlins gave her between her shoulder blades.

Andy was correct in feeling the penetration of blue eyes drilling the center of her departing back. Scott Rawlins was unhappy with the idea of a female pilot. He hesitated to fly with anyone anymore, even himself. Leftover fears from being shot down in Vietnam had curtailed his flying for years, but he was gradually getting back to it.

His discontent at the situation moved him to mutter to himself as he watched Andy walk away from him. Her father was the type of pilot he had in mind to make this trip, he thought, eyes narrowed. Not his whippersnapper daughter.

As if on cue, Avery Timmons headed out of the office toward a Cessna 152.

"Avery," Andy called and, as he turned to look back, she sprinted toward her father and the student who followed him. The strong breeze coming down out of the Rocky Mountains blew the coveralls back against her slender figure, giving Scott a good indication of nice curves underneath; small curves in the right places, distributed over her tall frame. The dark-streaked blond hair blew back from her tanned face in an out-of-style pixie cut that paid little attention to the wind always around the airfield, falling back into place no matter which way it went. It required little maintenance. Something she liked in a hairdo—and in all her planes.

Without a backward look at Mr. Rawlins and Jere,

she caught up with Avery, slipping her arm around his thickset waist.

"We have a slight hitch in the scheduled flight for Monday," she said, smiling at the young man beside them.

"Thought that was settled, hon," her father said, frowning. "You can easily be away all next week. I'll be home by Wednesday to help out."

"Yes, but Mr. Rawlins objects to a female pilot." She grinned up at her dad. "No offense, of course."

The expletive that came from Avery was one he used when faced with the prejudice that sometimes appeared when Andy was presented as the pilot of charter flights. It didn't seem to matter when the flight was a cargo shipment; perhaps as long as no human beings were involved, it was okay if the plane fell. If Air Service, Incorporated, wanted to trust a woman with a highly insured shipment, all right; but *not* with people.

Andy no longer resented it as much as she had at first. Now she was proud of her pilot's license and her Federal Aviation Authority approval for charter service. Besides, her dad had complete confidence in her to hold up her job with the family business.

She also held an aviation mechanic's certificate and would just as soon work on the planes as fly them. Anything to do with planes—she could do it all.

Avery and Jere were pilots, too, and Avery was the chief instructor. Andy helped when other duties allowed her. Jere was strictly the business end of the deal. He could fly, yes, but he didn't like to; in fact, he avoided it at all costs. Jere got deathly airsick. The

only way he could fly and not get airsick was if someone else piloted the craft and he took so many Dramamine tablets that he slept through the flight. It would
take a dire emergency for Jere to accept a schedule
that took him off the ground.

Avery stopped. "So what does Mr. Rawlins want to
do? Cancel?"

"Nope. He asked Jere to take the schedule."

Avery was watching his daughter, the crinkling at
the corner of her eyes lit now with laughter. He
grinned, shaking his head. "What'd Jere say?" he
asked.

She shrugged. "I didn't wait to find out."

"Go back and tell Mr. Rawlins how good you are
with planes, Andy," her dad said patiently. "Explain
you're better than Jere and me put together."

"Sure, Avery, you know he'll believe me, don't
you? He's going to take my word for it." Andy
watched her father pull the old aviation goggles out
and slide them over his silver-streaked hair. No one
but her dad would still use those things, but he swore
by them. Andy grinned affectionately as he waited for
his student to climb aboard; then Avery turned to her.

"Use your most convincing tactics, Andy. I trust
you." He swung up into the plane and she backed
away, waving to them. She watched the plane taxi
down the short runway, heading away from the highest peak of the mountains for takeoff.

It was a beautiful plane, bright blue and white, their
newest purchase for flight instruction. Breathing deeply of the clean fall air, she turned to lope back toward
the administration building.

As she entered the door, Jere and Mr. Rawlins were still standing just inside the building, both looking at her. Her narrow dark eyebrows peaked over her questioning eyes as she approached them.

"Everything settled to your satisfaction, Mr. Rawlins?" she inquired.

Jere could have kicked her and she knew it, but it was awfully hard to resist teasing a little when she saw doubt on a customer's face. Jere was her height, a year younger, but he outweighed her by a good fifty pounds. According to all statistics, he should be the pilot, the one who handled the planes with a innate skill. But it was his sister who possessed the knowledge and the love of planes and flying.

Jere—short for Jeremiah, a name he vehemently objected to—was the business brains behind the sales, contracts and all corporate duties. She and Avery gave those duties to him with their blessing. He posed no threat to their jobs, and they certainly had no designs on his.

"My mistake, Miss Timmons," Mr. Rawlins said. "I didn't realize you were the pilot of the outfit." He spoke pleasantly, but he really wanted to shake her. As the thought formed, he suddenly wondered how soft her straight shoulders would feel beneath his hands. Straightening in surprise at the outlaw thought, he met her glance.

"If you want to withdraw from the flight because of the misunderstanding, it can be arranged," Jere told him with a sidelong glance at Andy.

He shook his head. "That won't be necessary." He still watched Andy, who smiled her you're-my-favorite-customer smile for him. "May I speak to you about accommodations, Miss Timmons?"

The stiffness in his body caused her to wonder what accommodations he was about to request. "Of course, Mr. Rawlins. Right this way."

She led the way through another doorway into a small, neatly kept room. Seating herself behind one of the two desks, she pulled a ledger toward her, motioning at the same time for him to take one of the deeply cushioned leather chairs in front of the desk.

"Will a seven o'clock departure time be all right with you, Mr. Rawlins?" she asked, pen poised over a column of the ledger.

"I prefer eight," he said.

She nodded, checking the appropriate time box. "Destination is Great Falls, Montana?"

"Yes."

"When Jere talked with you last week, you weren't sure how many passengers would be going. Has that been decided?"

"There will be three of us," he told her, leaning forward. "Also, we'd like to take some cargo in addition to the luggage."

"As long as it doesn't weigh over two hundred pounds and is nonexplosive."

"It's about one hundred pounds of experimental hybrid grass seed for Miss Beakins's ranch," he explained. At her raised eyebrow, he added, "Miss Beakins is one of the passengers. The other one is Nolan Walters."

"I can go ahead and make out the manifest now

and have that much done, if you like. You can bring in the cargo Monday as long as you get here early enough to get it loaded before eight o'clock.''

He hesitated. ''Are you open on Sunday? I could leave it here overnight if you have room for it.''

''We aren't open Sundays, Mr. Rawlins; however, if you want to send it out here, I'll be around to accept it. The storage area is dry and the seed should be all right until Monday morning.''

''I don't want to put you to that much trouble....''

''No trouble,'' she assured him. ''I don't live far away.''

Reaching into the desk drawer, she took preprinted forms out and filled in the heading with his name. ''Your full name, Mr. Rawlins?''

''Scott H.''

I like that, she thought, drawing her upper lip down between her teeth. *Scott. Broad-shouldered; dependable. Ha! And he thinks little ladies should be home in the kitchen.*

''Your home address and phone number?'' As he recited it, she wrote without looking up at him. ''Do you have a business phone where we can reach you?'' He did, and she wrote the number down.

Checking other pertinent blanks down the page, she turned it over. ''I need the same information on the other two passengers, please.''

When she finished, she looked up and smiled, meeting the startling blue eyes with wide gray ones. ''That should do it. I look forward to seeing you on Monday, Mr. Rawlins.''

He frowned. ''How about Sunday with the seed?''

"Oh, I assumed someone else would deliver them," she said.

"No, I'll—"

The phone near her hand rang and she murmured, "Excuse me," and picked it up. "Air Service. Andy."

She listened for a moment and smiled. "Hi, Chuck. No, just going over the Luscombe to tighten it a little." Chuck Ransome was her only claim to a boyfriend, if he could be termed a boy. She was twenty-eight and Chuck was somewhere in the neighborhood of that same age. They both loved flying, skiing, eating her mother's cooking and being together every once in a while. She wasn't seriously in love with Chuck, and if he felt any differently he never showed it. President of the accounting firm that handled Air Service, Chuck kept Jere advised on all changes required to keep up with tax regulations.

"Sure, we're still going. I wasn't certain I'd be back, but it looks like they're returning Friday instead of Saturday, so I'll be home. Right. See you Saturday night." She hung up the phone and smiled apologetically at Mr. Rawlins.

"Sorry." She looked back at the papers. "The total for that flight with the cargo will be seventeen hundred dollars. That's one-way flights for two; two-way for one."

"Fine. Do you want the check now?" His eyes were on Andy's long fingers holding the pen. He had listened to her phone conversation and found himself wondering who this guy was she planned to see Saturday night.

She's fairly attractive, I guess, so why not a boyfriend,

he mused, wondering at the faint feeling of resentment he experienced as he heard her easy words with the unseen man. He came back to what Andy was telling him, staring into gray eyes that seemed to laugh at everything.

"Jere will take care of that for you. If you want to pay now and get rid of all preliminaries, that's fine. Otherwise, he can take it Monday."

"Now would be better, probably. Carla is always late and if she makes it by the skin of her teeth, I won't have time to write a check."

Smiling with understanding at the wiles of women, she led him through the doorway back to where her brother sat behind another desk.

"Mr. Rawlins is all set to leave Monday at eight o'clock, Jere," she said. "Take his money for me, would you?" She glanced at the daily work sheet posted behind his desk. "Is Lawrence on duty to go over the De Havilland behind me?"

"Yeah."

She threw another smile in Scott Rawlins's direction, only to find him staring at her, frowning slightly. "Something wrong?"

"Why is another person going over your plane?" he asked. If there was anything he wanted, it was the best checkout before he boarded a plane—especially with a female pilot.

"Lawrence is one of the best mechanics at Air Service. Two mechanics go over every plane that leaves here. Even the best of us can have a bad day, and we don't want you or your passengers endangered," she explained.

"Lawrence is one of the best? Why not the best one for our plane?" he asked.

"You have the best, Mr. Rawlins," she told him. "I'm it."

Gray eyes locked with icy blue for a moment; then she heard Jere laugh. The man in front of her turned toward her brother.

He gave a reluctant, wry grin. "You don't need to feel inferior because you can't fly, Jere," he said. "Your sister has enough confidence for everyone." *I should be so self-confident,* he wanted to say. *At one time, I felt the same way, and soon . . .* He cut off his thoughts.

"Jere doesn't feel inferior," she denied. "Anyone with brains to keep us in the black all these years has got to have something going in the brain department."

"As a businessman, I can agree wholeheartedly with that," Scott acknowledged, turning to leave.

"See you Mon— Sunday, Mr. Rawlins," Andy told him, leaning against Jere's desk to watch him stride away from them.

"Sunday?" Jere asked.

"Uh-huh. He's going to leave about one hundred pounds of experimental hybrid seed here Sunday. His girl friend is always late getting up and he's afraid it won't get aboard if he waits till Monday. I told him I'd store it for him."

"He was saying they plan to use the seed in some infertile land on Miss Beakins's ranch out near Great Falls. I hope it works."

"Even if it does, it's probably for the rich people. Who can afford specially grown hybrid grass seed to spread over thousands of acres of poor land?"

"Well, as long as they don't raise the taxes any more on our landing strip, we'll be okay, and stay away from grass seed."

She laughed. "You keep going to those town meetings and arguing, Jere. We need you." She turned to look out the window as the Cessna that Avery had taken out earlier came in for a smooth landing.

"Going to Mother's for dinner tonight, Andy?"

She shook her head. "No. I have a new record album I plan to listen to." Watching Avery swing across the field, she smiled. "How about you?"

"Fay and I are going to Morton's for dinner."

She nodded. One of these days those two would decide they couldn't live without each other and get married. Fay would be a decided plus to the Timmons family.

"See you in the morning, Jere. I'm scheduled out at seven o'clock." She strode out the door, long legs taking her around the corner of the building to an outside stairway. After taking the steps two at a time, she unlocked the heavy wooden door at the side of the small porch, leaving outside only the semblance of a plain administration building.

Inside, it was different. When she decided to take only the technical college training she needed for flying and not four years of regular courses, her dad had asked what she wanted done with the money he had saved for her education.

"Hey, Dad, let me tell you what I'd really like." When she told him, he grinned.

"Your idea has definite merit, Andy. Let's do it."

Over a period of two years, the three of them had used the money to build her an apartment over the offices of Air Service, Incorporated. She did it just the way she wanted it done and loved it.

Inside the heavy door she had just opened was an entranceway of terra-cotta tile in shaded hues of blue, beige and white. At the end of the tile, ice-blue carpet started, covering the entire area. She had divided the three-thousand-square-foot top floor into two rooms. To her right was the dining room and kitchen area. A trellis of green vines separated it from the living room. A long couch in a blue-and-beige print, a big matching chair, end tables and a huge slate-covered coffee table sat along one wall. A stereo sound system was installed with speakers arranged in various positions, albums and tapes placed neatly in slots and shelves. Over the stone mantel hung a latch-hook rug with a design of her pet Luscombe Silvaire plane done in silvers and blues. Her mother had crafted it from a drawing Fay made for her on web backing.

She crossed the spacious room to the bedroom door. Centered on the longest wall was a king-sized four-poster in the Paul Bunyan style, with huge rounded posts that took a while to dust when she got around to it. Over the bed was another of her mother's works: snow-covered peaks of the Rocky Mountains identical with the ones she could see from the bedroom window.

Comfortable, roomy and private. Besides, as she told Avery, I'm a good watchdog. There was a dependable security system, but her being on the premises made it doubly safe.

Flinging the windows open, she stood watching the gathering dusk of an early fall day. Dreamy-eyed, she watched as the first star appeared over the mountains, and she suddenly thought of Scott Rawlins. Her heart speeded up and she straightened at the unexpected feeling. She'd get to see him on Sunday and again on Monday. Well, so what, she asked herself, without an answer. In the meantime, she had a job to do tomorrow.

Sliding the zipper down the orange coveralls, she walked into the bathroom. It was so large that it held built-in chests of drawers, a dressing table the length of one wall and a sunken bath big enough for four people. Done in ceramic blue-and-beige tiles, it matched the decor throughout the apartment.

Sitting nude on the side of the tub, she stared into the water as it filled, letting her hand drift along the top. Then when the water reached the desired temperature, she submerged her body. She had some medical equipment to deliver down at Durango tomorrow and would be back before dark. Saturday she could work on the Silvaire, and Sunday she'd see Scott Rawlins. She frowned. Why should that matter?

She shrugged. He was good-looking; that should be reason enough. He also had the oddest-colored hair she had ever seen on a man. And he didn't seem to be that old.

She stared at her red toenails sticking out of the water and a sensation foreign to her tightened every muscle in her body.

Well, she thought in surprise, *suddenly I can't wait to find out more about Scott Rawlins.*

Chapter Two

The Cessna 421 was ready for takeoff. Its sleek silver paint trimmed in orange glittered in the early-morning light. Andy waved to Jere, swinging her long body up into the plane.

Two medical technicians were already strapped into the comfortable seats, and she smiled at them as she settled into the cockpit. The X-ray equipment being shipped to the hospital in Durango was secured. She taxied to Baker runway, waiting for the go-ahead from Lawrence. Visibility was ten miles, weather clear and a bit nippy for this early in the fall.

Lawrence signaled her and she eased the throttle up, gliding smoothly. One more radio check, one more thumbs up, and the plane rolled down the runway, lifting at exactly the precise moment she meant it to. She smiled to herself, glancing down at the forested carpet below her and the mountains to her right.

She headed south and relaxed for the flight. Two hours later, a smooth landing put her down at the small airport outside Durango.

While the X-ray equipment was unloaded and

taken to the hospital, the technicians ate lunch. Andy
meanwhile wandered around the narrow streets of the
picturesque town. At the drugstore that still boasted a
soda fountain, she ordered a chocolate milk shake and
chatted with Mrs. Byron, the owner. Keeping her eyes
on her watch, she timed her trip back to the airport
with the shuttle bus she knew went out there regu-
larly.

With perfect weather ahead, she nosed the Cessna
over the six-thousand-foot mountains toward Longmont. Climbing to eighteen thousand feet, she followed the scenic route north across the area of Lake
City into the lower ranges of the mountains. Flying
east across the end of the Sangre de Cristo Range of
the Rockies, she swung straight north, west of the
Denver airways, over Boulder into Longmont. The
sun was hanging at the top of the highest peak of
mountains to her left as she dropped onto the runway,
taxiing into the marked slot Jere was directing her to.

"Got a ride waiting?" she asked the first hospital
technician to depart from the plane.

"Yes, thanks, Andy." The two of them waved to
her as they ran the short distance to a station wagon
with hospital lettering on the side.

"Put it in the barn for me, Jere?"

"Right. Good trip?" Her brother waited to see her
nod and turned to put the plane in the hangar. He
didn't get airsick in a plane as long as he stayed on the
ground.

Poor Jere, she thought. He loved to fly and hated it
at the same time. Thankfully, she never got airsick.

Andy finished filling out her papers for the trip and

signing all the logs. Pulling all the receipts from her pockets to leave for Jere to post, she ran up the outside steps to her apartment. As she let herself in, she leaned for a moment against the door. It was a simply decorated room, but done in such a way that it reflected quiet grace.

The phone rang as she crossed the room, and she dropped on to the floor to sit cross-legged as she answered it. "Hello? Oh, hi, Mother," she said.

"Would you like to come for dinner, Andy? Jere and Fay will be here and there's plenty."

"Thanks, Mother, maybe Sunday night if you're having some good leftovers."

"Andy," her mother chided. "The leftovers won't be good Sunday evening."

She laughed. "I meant Sunday leftovers. There won't be any tonight with Jere there to eat."

"Well, then, why not Sunday dinner?" her mother asked.

"There's a customer coming to deliver cargo and I have to be around the field for a while. I don't have an exact time, so I don't know when he'll be there."

"Bring him for dinner," her mother insisted. *Good ol' mother.* Andy grinned to herself. She'll feed anyone who'll eat.

"Not a chance, Mother," she said. "He's not about to associate with a female pilot, of all things. He doesn't even want to fly with me."

Her mother's quiet laughter told her she understood. "He'll change his mind after his trip, Andy. You know how men are about women in a *man's* domain, for goodness' sake."

"Yep, I sure do."

After a few moments, her mother agreed to save her a bite to eat for Sunday evening. She hung up the phone and sat rubbing her fingers through the thick pile of the carpet.

Almost the color of Scott Rawlins's eyes, she thought. Her eyebrows peaked and she made a clicking sound with her tongue. She'd remembered more things about Mr. Rawlins in a day than she did about most of the passengers that she flew with in a week.

"Odd," she murmured aloud. "Must be the strange color of his hair and his eyes."

With the stereo on and an evening alone ahead of her, she picked up the aviation trade journals she seldom had time to read. Sliding between sheets the same color blue as the carpet, she propped two pillows beneath her head and opened the first magazine on top of the pile. But she didn't get far when sleep overtook her.

When she awoke, it was morning.

Perfect waste of time, she thought, standing at the window with a cup of coffee. She did it so few times that it didn't bother her. Rested and feeling vibrant at the dawn of a beautiful new day, she dressed in the work uniform for Saturday—her favorite orange coveralls.

Downstairs, she opened everything and put on coffee for Jere and Avery. They usually didn't show up until around eight-thirty, expecting coffee to be ready when they appeared.

The schedule said she had a lesson set up for nine,

the Norton girl. A natural when it came to the controls of the plane, Kimberly Norton was a sophomore at the University of Colorado. She wanted to be a flight attendant for one of the major airlines, but Andy was gently undermining that, pointing her instead toward a commercial pilot's training.

Wouldn't Mr. Rawlins's beautiful silver locks stand on end if he knew about that?

Him again, she thought. What is this?

"Hi, Andy," a breathless voice behind her said.

Smiling as she turned, Andy waved to Kimberly Norton and strode to meet the girl. Up in the air a few minutes later, she turned the controls over to Kim and sat back to observe her moves in the cockpit. The tight features of the Citabria responded and they climbed above the lower mountain ridges, staying in their approved lanes for training.

Thirty minutes later, Kim dropped the plane on the runway in a perfect landing. "Getting better all the time, Kim," Andy told her.

They walked toward the administration building, and she could see Avery talking to two men outside the main door.

"Andy," Kim was saying, "you know what you were telling me about piloting for a commercial business or even for airlines?"

"Yes."

"I talked to my dad about it. He says Louisiana Tech has a great school for getting the credits I need to finish up my senior year. That is, if I want to transfer down there after next year."

"He's right, but during your spring break or next

summer, why don't you take a hop down there and look it over? That's the best way to do it. I spent a year there myself."

"Did you like it?" Kim asked eagerly.

Andy laughed. "I was homesick."

"Really?"

She looked around. "It's a lot different from here, Kim. It's hot and humid. Or cold and humid." She grinned at the younger girl. "The people and the food are great; the weather is best not even talked about. But as far as the school and its curriculum, you can't beat it for our field."

"Well . . ."

"If you have all your math and science credits, Kim, you won't have any problems. They stress those studies, plus the technical and theoretical training they give there. And when I say stress, I mean it. You go through intense, thorough training. Equipment; weather; anything that will affect the vehicle you're flying, whether it's a small plane, a jumbo jet or a helicopter."

Kim was listening with something like horror. "What if I ever flunk after all this studying here and lessons?"

Andy grinned down at the shorter girl. "Not a chance, if you study like you've done here. You can handle it. Tell you what. I still have all my books with drills and exercises in them. I'll drag them out and have them ready for you next lesson."

"Oh, boy, I'd love to see them." It was Kim's turn to tease. "Still got your grades on them?"

"Probably. I'll hide the ones where I flunked." She

touched Kim's arm. "You have a few months to think it over. Since your parents are in favor of it, do whatever you want to do. It's a big decision; it's definitely a good school."

Promising to show up the next Saturday, Kim ran to her car. Andy walked in the direction of Avery and the men with whom he was talking.

"Got a moment, Andy?" Avery called as she came abreast of them.

"Sure, Avery, for you, anytime." She hooked her arm through his as she faced the two men. She stiffened as she stared into the blue eyes of Scott Rawlins.

"You remember Mr. Rawlins?" At her nod he said, "And this is Nolan Walters."

Andy nodded to Mr. Rawlins and held her hand out to the other man. "Mr. Walters," she acknowledged.

Her dad looked at her as he went on. "I know you were looking forward to an easy day, but these two gentlemen want to know if you can take them to Grand Junction."

Why that doubting— He's checking up to see if I really know how to fly before he trusts me across a couple of states. She grinned. *If that's the way he wants to spend his money, fine.*

"Sure, Dad." Andy gave each of the men a friendly smile. She saw an odd gleam in Scott Rawlins's eyes for an instant, and then it was gone. "What do you want me to fly?"

"Take the Beechcraft since you have no cargo. I'll get Lawrence to get it ready for takeoff."

"Half an hour, gentlemen?" she asked.

"That will be fine," Mr. Rawlins said, watching her closely.

She nodded to all three of them and went toward the office to fill Jere in on the paperwork that would need to be done.

"You believe that?" she asked her brother. "What he's doing is trying to see if I really know how to fly before he takes his precious lady friend up with me."

Jere grinned at her. "Now, Andy, surely he wouldn't risk a friend in favor of a lady." He clicked his tongue. "Haven't you already pegged him as a male chauvinist?"

"Sort of," she admitted. Jere knew his sister quite well. "But the lady in question is probably so beautiful it's unbearable—and rich, besides, to own a ranch up in Montana, flying up to test a few grass seeds."

She leaned her arms on the counter, gray eyes going pensively to the misty blue of the mountains in the distance. "How was Mother's dinner last night?"

He didn't look up from the papers he was filling out. "You know what her lasagne's like. Why torture yourself?"

"Maybe you left me enough to stick in the microwave?" she asked hopefully.

"Not a chance, Andy. You should have come out." He was absolutely unsympathetic.

"Well," she said, feigning disgust, "I didn't need those extra calories anyway."

"A few wouldn't hurt you, however," a voice behind her said.

She turned a polite smile to Scott Rawlins. "Mother doesn't cook so that anyone can stop with a *few* calories, Mr. Rawlins," she said. "Her lasagne is a thousand per bite."

Jere laughed, trying to disguise some of the sting in Andy's words. "She's right." He nodded. "But goo-oo-d," he added.

"The 'Craft is ready, Andy," Lawrence called from the doorway.

Andy had gone over the log and manifest, checking the purpose of the flight. Business interests, the block indicated. Monkey, no doubt, she thought to herself. But flying was her business and she didn't care what they did as long as they could pay for the trip.

SCOTT WATCHED the swing of Andy's slim figure ahead of him as they crossed toward the plane Lawrence had checked out for her. Since the slight mixup about who was to pilot their plane on Monday, his thoughts seemed to take a perverse pleasure in returning to Andy at rather odd times.

At dinner with Carla the night before, he was studying the menu he knew by heart. A pair of gray eyes, mocking laughter shining up at him, appeared over the wine list.

"What did you say, Scott?"

He looked across at Carla. She was going over the wine list, but a frown formed between her eyes. "Nothing. Just wishing they'd change these dishes around occasionally to give us something new to look at."

He used the fact that he was trying to get a flight the next morning to end their evening early. He was tired, for one thing.

Carla questioned him only a little. "Are you beginning to feel more at ease in a plane, Scott? I thought we were doing well to get you to fly up to the ranch. Now you're scheduling a flight on the same weekend."

It was not strange that she wondered. Uneasiness about flying had kept him grounded for years, but little by little he was getting back into the air. The nightmares of Vietnam were receding.

"Nolan and I need to get over to Grand Junction now to check a scheduling at the lodge. A flight is the only way we can squeeze it into our work in time to make any necessary changes."

Actually, Scott could have squeezed it in anytime, since he ran his business from either the office or from home, whichever was convenient for him. A generous inheritance from his grandmother gave him a head start on most people and a sharp business acumen turned it into a small fortune.

Part of his inheritance had been land where the Terrence Hills section now stood. Condominiums and town houses were built on it only after he was assured fifty-percent ownership of the restaurant constructed there. The golf course was his exclusively. He found that dealing in real estate came naturally for him, and profits couldn't be argued with.

Looking at the menu, he shrugged away his thoughts of Andy Timmons. She was the first woman to enter his thoughts more than once since he and Carla had agreed to be unengaged several months before.

ANDY'S PREPARATIONS for the flight to Grand Junction were automatic, but her usual concentration was broken by thoughts of Scott Rawlins. Shaking away the wayward thinking, she bent to the task at hand, forcing herself to work at the job that was usually more or less routine. She never took chances that everything was right; she made sure they were, and today could be no exception. She was ready for the trip.

The Beechcraft she piloted was an older but dependable aircraft and she loved the way it handled. She found the flight pattern easily and set the controls, automatically checking instruments and outside terrain. She crossed the mountains at their lowest point and more or less followed the scenic highway toward Grand Junction. At one-fifteen, she banked over Grand Junction and landed at Walker Field.

She filed her flight plan to depart at four-thirty and thought about what she wanted for lunch.

"Miss Timmons?"

She turned, smiling her best businesslike smile, to face Scott Rawlins. "Yes?"

"Nolan and I are going to drive over to Palisade and have lunch there. Would you like to come with us?"

"No, thanks. I'll wait for you here." She wanted to ask if his stomach was solid enough to eat, but thought better of it. The flight had been smooth. Neither man commented on the trip. They appeared engrossed in their own discussions, seemingly content to let her handle the plane.

They drove away in a rented car, and she went into the coffee shop to order a sandwich. Someone had left a morning paper on the counter, and she picked it up to look over the advertisements. Powderhorn Ski Area was advertising its coming season.

That's near Palisade, she thought. Maybe Scott and his friend were preparing for the coming snows. Andy loved to ski. She and Chuck didn't take to the most sophisticated runs but they managed to enjoy the smaller ones around Hidden Valley. At least they didn't have to go so far to ski, not much over a hundred miles. She would hate to have to fly two hours every time she wanted to go skiing, she thought, placing the paper back where she found it.

She caught a ride into Grand Junction with one of the men she knew from the airfield and went to the bookstore. She had all the aviation journals so settled for a crossword-puzzle magazine. She took a taxi back to Walker Field and settled down to wait for her passengers.

As Scott Rawlins and Nolan Walters walked back into the room where she was waiting, Andy looked at her watch. Good timing, she thought with approval. People who file flight plans didn't like to have to change them.

"You must get bored sitting around waiting for people," Mr. Walters said.

She looked at him and smiled. He was several inches shorter than Scott Rawlins, with sandy hair thinning on top and brown eyes behind steel-framed glasses.

"Very seldom, Mr. Walters," she assured him.

"Why don't you call me Nolan?" he asked. "We may see a lot of each other."

If this works out, she finished for him. It was almost funny the way you could see their devious little minds working, she thought, moving away toward the door.

Scott Rawlins didn't speak until they were entering the plane. As she stood to the side with Griff, one of the mechanics from Walker Field, he stopped in front of her.

"What time are we due back, Andy?" he asked.

"Approximately six-fifteen, Mr. Rawlins," she said.

Griff touched her arm as he moved away. "I'll get you aloft, Andy, and see you next time around." She nodded, still looking at her passenger, who hadn't moved.

"Perhaps you should call me Scott instead of being so formal," he said. The blue eyes went over her—the windblown hair, tanned face slim almost to the point of being gaunt, gray eyes narrowed in the afternoon brilliance. Only a few inches shorter than his six feet two, her straight slender figure revealed few curves beneath the loose coveralls.

Scott enjoyed the play of expression over Andy's face as his eyes rested there once more. She was cute, in a girl-next-door sort of fashion. Smiling at the questioning look on her face, he boarded the plane ahead of her.

"I'll do that," she said and swung up behind him to settle into the cockpit.

Moments later, airborne, she let her thoughts reach ahead to the dance she was attending with Chuck that night. Their flight club had a monthly square dance, well attended by pilots, would-be pilots, mechanics and friends.

Without incident, she brought the plane in and left it for Jere to secure it for the night.

"We appreciate your taking us on such short notice, Andy," Scott said from behind her.

"No problem," she said, her voice pleasant. "I hope having a female pilot wasn't too bad on your digestion."

Nolan gave a booming laugh. "I guess you're used to flak from people like Scott, are you?"

She shook her head. "No, as a matter of fact, I never get used to it."

Scott's head jerked up and his eyes narrowed as he met her look. "Perhaps you should try getting over being so thin-skinned about it, then," he said, his voice definitely on the cool side.

"That's what my mother tells me," she said agreeably.

For a moment, she thought she saw the suggestion of a smile in his eyes, but it was gone instantly.

They glared quite frankly at each other for a moment before he said, rather stiffly, "I'll bring the shipment around about five o'clock tomorrow if that's all right with you."

"That's a good time. I'll be here." She watched them leave and turned to look at Jere, who wiped the grin from his face as she stomped from the room. *Why I let it bother me when someone new decides I'm out of place is beyond me,* she muttered to herself as she went up the steps to her apartment. Especially Scott Rawlins. Playboy or rich somebody, a girl friend rolling in money from the sounds of her dealings: experimental grass seed, flying all over the country, and heaven only knows what else.

Oh, well, she decided, shrugging out of her coveralls. Some of us must work for a living. *And what would I do without flying?* She stretched her long lean body toward the high ceiling of her living room and admitted to herself she'd never want to change places with anyone she knew.

Chapter Three

Her outfit for the Saturday night affair was new: a pale-yellow blouse, with long, full sleeves, that matched a darker-yellow-print tiered skirt. The crinoline petticoats she wore underneath caused the skirt to swing out and show a great amount of long leg, as she noticed when she tried it on. She had plenty of leg to show; at least it was shapely, Chuck informed her.

The dance was in the spacious hall of their flight club, which boasted a band made up of local members. Jere did some of the calling, then Chuck took over for a while. It was a bigger crowd than usual, Andy decided as she stood near the bar. Chuck was off somewhere discussing accounting or flying or skiing—any number of worthwhile subjects.

"Hello, Andy."

A vibrant shock went through her before she turned to face Scott Rawlins. Her eyes took in the almost rumpled silver hair and smiling blue eyes, down to the blue plaid Western-style shirt he wore tucked into darker-blue pants.

Without warning, her heart shifted into fifth gear

and raced away from her. She drew in her breath. "Hello, Scott."

At his smile, she blinked and her gaze settled on the woman by his side. *If Scott's an eyeful, take a look at what's with him*, her inner self instructed.

"I'd like you to meet Carla Beakins, Andy," he said. "She'll be flying with us to Great Falls on Monday."

At least five inches shorter than Andy, Carla Beakins nevertheless stood regally beside Scott. Her honey-blond hair was pulled loosely back from her face and fastened into a chignon low on her neck. Creamy-white cheeks, touched lightly with a blusher, were offset by a pale-red lipstick, outlining perfectly shaped lips.

The gown she wore was intended to be worn at the by-invitation-only balls around Denver in the high society season. It was not suitable for square dancing. A thin strap barely held the red satin material to her shoulders, lowering it provocatively to the cleft between softly rounded breasts. It clasped her small waist so tightly Andy wanted to take a deep breath for her. From the tiny waist it flared over shapely hips, inviting the touch of a caressing hand.

Andy swallowed, trying not to stare at the picture before her. Scott Rawlins was enthralled, and no wonder. She met the woman's cool glance, startled that her wide eyes were amber-colored, like marbles in the sun.

Conscious of impolite staring, Andy smiled and said, "Hello, Miss Beakins."

The amber eyes dismissed the tall, gangly woman

in front of her as she turned to Scott. "If you think the bartender knows how to mix a Scotch and water, I'd love one."

· *Snob* was Andy's first thought, but she kept her smile intact as she shook her head in answer to Scott's question about her drink preference.

She opened her mouth to make conversation, but Carla was looking across the dance floor. Following her gaze, Andy's eyes narrowed as she saw that Carla's amber eyes were fastened on Jere, standing with his arm across Fay's shoulders.

Amber eyes that wander, she thought cattily as Scott came back to hand the drink to Carla.

"Thanks, Scott," she murmured without looking at him. "Who's the good-looking cowboy with Rebecca of Sunnybrook Farm?" she asked.

"My brother," Andy told her. "And watch it. Where Jere's concerned, Rebecca has claws a mile long." She nodded to Scott, who grinned at her warning, and walked away from them.

Andy could feel her face stinging from the anger that swept her body at Carla's comment. Aside from being a snob, she thought she was God's gift to society.

Well, an inner voice said testily, *you said she must be really something; rich, gorgeous, owns Scott Rawlins body and soul. . . .* She cut off her thoughts with the sharpest indrawn breath she could. *Stop bringing Scott into every thought you have, Andy, my love,* she admonished herself, and went right on with her thoughts. No wonder he's captivated. She's about as beautiful as any one woman could be.

The band was tuning instruments, the raucous sound making conversation difficult. She stopped to speak to Fay and Jere, leaning toward them to be heard.

Jere wore a wide grin. "I invited Scott to come but sure didn't think he would." His gaze lingered on the stately looking couple across the room. "Boy, that Carla is really something, isn't she?"

Fay followed his look and, for a moment, said nothing. Then she touched his arm to get at his attention.

"She is something, Jere, but *not* for you." She poked him in the ribs to emphasize her point. He smiled down at her and kissed her turned-up nose. Fay was small, her figure more like that of a fourteen-year-old than of someone of twenty-five. With black hair and almost black eyes, her unusually fair skin contrasted sharply with eyes and hair. She had moved into Jere's life two years ago when the company she worked for relocated in Longmont from Greeley. Chuck, the accountant for the firm, introduced them. If they had been separated since that time, Andy couldn't remember when it was.

In a fight between Fay and Carla, I'd side with Fay, Andy thought. *Carla might learn a few things from Rebecca if she fooled with Jere.*

The screeching of tuning instruments faded and music sounded in the room. Andy continued on around the room, keeping her eyes open to locate Chuck.

"Looking for me?"

She turned to smile up at him. "Yes, as a matter of fact. Thought I'd been deserted." Her eyes went over the familiar figure. He was probably an inch taller than she was, thick through the shoulders, resembling a lumberjack as much as anything else. He was easygoing and knew everyone in town. His eyes were brown and his dark-brown hair was styled a little too long, she thought, for someone his age. But that was his business. He didn't criticize her and she didn't try to tell him what to do.

I guess that's why we've been together this long, she thought suddenly as she watched him. He asked her to marry him about twice a year, and twice a year she turned him down. She frowned now, wondering why. She really liked him. But—love him?

When his kisses became a little too demanding for her, she withdrew. She enjoyed the light petting and touching occasionally, but when his breath grew ragged, she backed away. Only once did she remember his becoming upset over her refusal to indulge in sex play.

They had been skiing and were lying on the floor of their cabin in front of the fire. Half asleep, she smiled as he rolled over and pushed her hair back from her face.

"You're so lovely, Andy," he whispered. He bent his head to kiss her, and as she moved her lips beneath his, he pulled her over on him, holding her body against him. For a moment, she responded to him; then she tried to pull away. He held on, a groan coming from deep in his chest as he kept her lips crushed to his.

She mumbled, trying to free herself, but he wouldn't let her go. Finally, she freed one hand enough to lock it in his hair and yanked until he let her go with an oath.

"What the hell's going on, Andy?" he demanded. He sat up, glaring at her, then shook his head as he got to his feet. "What's wrong with you, anyway? You love me, don't you? Is it so hard to understand that you drive me crazy, pushing me away all the time?"

She stared at him, realizing he was right. She didn't want him to get too close to her at all. Light kisses, a few touches, but after that—no. Just no.

Chuck didn't know why she was that way, but she could have told him. It was something she was still reluctant to remember. Something that had happened when she was dating a man who frequently used their charter service.

She liked him and when he held her close, whispering to her, his hands stroking places no man had ever touched, she trembled with unexplained feelings. Movies told how great the emotions were that involved sexual satisfaction; television programs were rampant with sexy scenes that depicted ecstasy when men and women belonged completely to each other.

And one night, they went far enough for her to find out for herself. When he teased her until she was tormented with desire, she gave in, and as he made all the sounds supposed to mean enjoyment, she lay stiff with pain. There was nothing fulfilling about submitting to physical desires; all she felt was stinging discomfort, a powerful need to be finished and get away from the hurt she was experiencing.

That was six years ago, and she hadn't let anyone get that close to her again. If that was sexual enjoyment and satisfaction, she could certainly do without it. Chuck was the one suffering from her aversion to the joyous union between male and female touted in song and story.

Now she stood looking at Chuck, knowing she was unfair to him. He was always around, taking her places—skiing, ice skating. Aside from her company and a light good-night kiss, he came up empty-handed. She had told him this on occasion, but he only laughed at her.

"I may get pushy every once in a while, Andy, but I know you're going to stop me. Why should I deprive myself of your great company even if you are cool to my propositions?"

"I'm not ready to get married, Chuck," she told him one night when he proposed. "I may be old enough, but I'm just not ready. If and when I marry, it's going to be forever, and I can't afford to be premature in this case."

"I know," he told her, patting her cheek, then sticking his hands in his pockets. "I have to keep my bid in, though, in case you decide to marry one day. I want to be there."

"You're sweet."

"Nope, Andy, just stubborn." They had laughed together and the awkward moment passed.

She seldom thought about marriage, even to Chuck. As she said, she just wasn't ready, and there was plenty of time for such permanent alliances on down the road of life somewhere.

The band struck up a tentative hop, then went smoothly into "Cotton-Eyed Joe." The music faded, and the master of ceremonies for the evening got up to alert everyone to the first dance of the night. A moment later, they were all on the floor, and Chuck swung her into the circle.

With the "aleman left" call, Chuck swung her and turned her loose. At the end of the twirl, she was caught around the waist, and with crossed arms, she found herself partnered with Scott Rawlins. She smiled, the damp rosiness of her lips catching for a second between her teeth. There was a thin film of perspiration on his forehead, and she noticed for the first time how white his teeth were against the tan of his face.

Summers in the country clubs and winters on the ski slopes, the life of the idle rich, she thought. He had a business, but what kind? She had no idea. Jere would probably know from records he had to make of passengers chartering flights out of state.

He started to speak about the time they changed partners and she was whirled away. When the music stopped, she was out of breath and standing near Jere. Fay was across the room holding on to Chuck and laughing up at him.

"How about a drink, Andy?" Jere asked.

"You buying?"

"Flip you for it," he said, laughing.

"Cheapskate."

He pulled a coin from his pocket and flipped it. "Heads," she said as it landed on the back of his hand.

"Tails," he said triumphantly.

Shrugging gracefully, she walked over to the bar and gave orders for them, including one for Fay.

"Here you are, Andy. Watch out for the most potent drink in the house," the man behind the bar told her.

"I will," she promised, handing Jere the drinks for him and Fay. She sipped her rich orange concoction, enjoying the cool tangy taste as it went down her dry throat. She watched Jere cross the room to where Fay stood with Chuck.

"Pilots aren't supposed to drink much, are they?" a cool voice inquired, and she turned to face Scott.

"I don't have a flight till Monday," she said. "I should be sober by then, wouldn't you think?"

He glanced around. "How long do these shindigs last?"

Tongue in cheek, she said, "Depends."

His gaze came back to her. "On what?"

"How involved everyone gets; how much drinking they do; really, how long the participants want to make it last. If you're having a good time, you wouldn't mind staying, would you?" She couldn't resist adding, "Or is Miss Beakins already bored?"

He half turned away from her and she followed the direction of his look. Carla stood with a small hand on Jere's arm, gazing up at him as though he were the King of Jordan. Jere looked completely bewitched, and Andy felt a tiny misgiving. Fay stood to one side, taking in the little tête-à-tête.

"Likes to play, does she?" Andy asked, letting her tongue slide along her lower lip. "Is this the way she keeps from getting bored?"

"Carla's harmless," Scott said, his voice cool. "Don't worry about your brother."

"But I do," she said. "He's younger and doesn't yet know about *all* kinds of women."

A slight smile touched his mouth, and Andy found it hard to look away from the firm flesh. With a mental shake, she turned to look across the room again. Fay had moved between Jere and Carla, her back deliberately to the beautiful woman. Jere put his drink on the table beside them and took Fay in his arms as the music started again, leaving Carla standing at the edge of the crowd.

She could see the cancellation of Monday's flight coming, she thought, seeing anger clearly stamped on Carla's face. Before her indrawn breath could be completed, Scott touched her arm.

"May I?" Without waiting for an answer, he took her drink and set it on the bar behind them. A moment later, he whirled her across the floor.

Most square dances give few opportunities to be held close, and this was one of the things Andy liked about them the most. Right now, she would have liked to be dancing a waltz just to see how it felt to be close to Scott's lean, hard body. With an effort, she concentrated on following the fast steps. They both were out of breath when the music stopped.

Laughing at the improvisations of a couple near them on the floor, she looked at Scott to find his compelling blue eyes going over her face and hair. Self-consciously, she lifted one hand to push the hair back from her face.

Without a word, he finished his perusal of her features, his gaze lingering once more on her mouth before he met her eyes. The slight frown on his face gave way to a slow smile and she stiffened as her heart flipped.

She knew she was acting like a moonstruck teen-ager, for goodness' sake. He was definitely not the best-looking man she'd ever seen—but close. She bit her lip.

Pacing her breathing, she returned his smile and turned to search for Chuck. He was deep in animated conversation with a couple she recognized as business acquaintances.

"Ransome a friend of yours?" Scott asked, following her gaze.

"Yes."

"More than a friend?"

Facing fully toward him, she asked, "How can someone be more than a friend, Scott?" Her gray eyes locked for a moment with eyes the color of the sky over the Rockies at about six o'clock on a clear fall morning. Something long repressed inside of her stirred and came to life. Feelings long denied rose above the protective wall she had built. A warning whisper raised danger flags along her spine. A whisper that didn't reach the sharp thrill that started in the pit of her stomach and slid sensuously into her thighs.

He nodded as though he understood what was going through her mind at the moment. But he didn't. If he did, he'd be the one to cancel the flight on Monday instead of Carla.

"May I?" Chuck asked, touching her arm.

"Oh, Chuck, have you met Scott Rawlins?"

Chuck grinned. "Scott and I know each other." He stuck out his hand. "How are you, Scott?"

She stood aside as the two men exchanged pleasant-
ries, glad for the chance to get her thoughts back into
line. Chuck was the outgoing type, a definite plus in
his work as chief accountant for his own firm, and
could carry a conversation without any trouble at all.
In direct contrast to her. She had to have something to
talk about—flying, for instance.

A hand slid with easy familiarity around her narrow
waist. "How about this dance, gorgeous?"

Eye to eye, she faced Jere. "I've already been
asked."

"Go ahead, Andy,"' Chuck said. "I guess your
brother's allowed one dance."

"Cripple Creek," in the Grand Ol' Opry style, had
couples swinging in rowdy rhythm around the floor.
Jere swung Andy with ease and, as the dance ended,
she was back in his arms where she started.

Breathless, she leaned against him. "I may be getting too old for this," she told him.

"You'd better be getting in shape for skiing," he
said, laughing and out of breath, too. "According to
the caterpillars, we're going to have a long, cold
winter."

Raising her eyebrows, she asked, "When did you
talk to a knowledgeable caterpillar?"

"Scott brought an almanac with him the other day,
and I was looking through it. It had an article in it
about the hybrid grass seed they're experimenting
with." His eyes left her face to search the crowd. She
knew exactly when his eyes contacted those of Carla
Beakins. "Interesting," he murmured.

One long forefinger poked into his solid-muscled

arm. "Poisons are also interesting. Also something to stay away from after you've read the instructions."

He turned back to grin at her. "And the instructions?" He didn't pretend to know what she meant.

"Read carefully, then destroy," she said.

He laughed, reaching for Fay as she came up to them. She felt a lot easier as she saw the look that passed between the two.

The music started and Chuck turned her into his arms. Between the whirls and dips of the fast-paced dance, she saw Jere, Fay and Scott talking until Carla joined them, pulling Scott away with a small possessive hand on his arm. Curbing the tiny slither of dislike she felt, she concentrated on enjoying the dance.

"Be back in a minute, Andy," Chuck told her as he stationed her near the bar again, handing her the drink she had left there.

Nodding, she glanced around the room, knowing Chuck was on his way to talk business or the coming ski season with someone from the city council or with one of his club or golf buddies. He knew everyone. The band was on a break, and groups of people stood around talking, drinking and generally enjoying themselves.

Wiping the dampness from her glass with a napkin, she sauntered around the end of the bar through the side exit to stand by the second-floor balcony. This was her favorite time of year—cool, but not cold. Dry and pleasant. She loved the snow, too, but . . .

"Abandoned?" Scott asked from behind her.

She was leaning with her back against the banister, elbows lying across it, holding her drink in her right hand. A half turn of her head brought her face to face with him. The brightness of the nearly full moon lit his features, casting shadows along one cheek.

"Not really," she said, her voice lazy. "I never feel abandoned as long as I can see the Rockies."

"Why's that?" he asked, looking away from her toward the shadows of the mountains.

"When I'm flying, as long as I have the mountains to the west of me, I'm not far from home."

"But you're not flying."

She tipped her head back to look up at the stars. "The mountains are still to the west of me, so I'm close to home."

He laughed lightly and she lowered her gaze to look at him. His firm lips parted to reveal even white teeth. As his eyes narrowed with laughter, tiny crinkles appeared and the blue depths reflected the starlight.

"Chuck assures me that you seldom get lost on any flights," he said, watching her closely.

It was her turn to laugh lightly. "Did you need that assurance, Scott?" Taking a sip of her drink, she turned toward the balcony, propping her hip against it for balance.

He didn't answer right away and she questioned him with widened eyes. He was closer to her than she thought, and she could see the darkening skin where his beard had grown. The moonlight on his hair turned it to silver with a bluish tint. Shadowy lashes lay against his cheeks as he looked down at her.

"I didn't ask him; he volunteered. I guess he thought I might wonder a little. You don't meet women charter pilots in your normal-day activities."

Facing away from him once more, she said, "I guess not, although you'll be seeing more and more as prejudices such as yours disappear."

"I didn't mean to be prejudiced. Surprised is more the word I would use. When the name Andy was mentioned as the pilot for our flight, naturally—"

"You don't have to explain all this to me, Scott. I've heard it several hundred times."

Scott had no intention of explaining anything to her. He made ordinary conversation, but only to give himself time to look over the woman in front of him. She was so in control, so confident of herself when it came to flying. As he had once been—and would be again soon, he was certain.

"Andy?" The odd inflection in his voice brought her head around. He reached for the glass in her hand and bent to place it on the balcony at their feet. As he straightened, he took her into his arms.

Surprise held her still for a moment. Then, drawing in a sharp breath, she took a step backward. His step forward brought their bodies together and she was caught between Scott and the banister she had been leaning on.

Her head went back as she looked up, intent on stopping his embrace. Instead, his head lowered quickly and his lips caught hers.

"N—" The denial was never uttered as his mouth closed over hers. The fusion of starlight and darkness beneath her closed lids kept her still in his arms. His mouth explored hers, parting her lips when she would have kept them closed. This was where she always stopped Chuck, where she drew the line. The feelings coming from the touch of Scott's lips were not ones she remembered when Chuck kissed her. They built their own fires inside her and flames licked through her body.

Her hands pushing against his chest let up and went around his neck. The tips of her fingers touched the line where thick hair had been trimmed behind his ears. At the same time, his hand cupped her hip beneath the fullness of her skirt, pressing her into his hard thighs. She wanted to withdraw from him, wanted to stop his exploring mouth.

Twisting her head, she freed her mouth, opening it to protest, only to find his tongue inside, plundering recklessly. Sliding her hands down his chest, she pushed without success. Dropping them to his waist, she dug her fingers into his shirt, bunching it, trying to get a hold on his flesh. Slowly, she became aware of not wanting to stop him; not wanting to stem the tide that washed through her body; wanting the sensations he stirred into life to go on and on.

As though drugged, she gave him her lips without questioning the reason, leaning into him to allow his caresses, aware of his hands stroking her shoulders, finally coming up so that they cupped the back of her head.

Words of an old love song wafted through her consciousness and the fragrance of the fall night closed in on them. Even after his mouth moved from hers to touch her eyelids, she remained tightly molded to his body, holding him, her hands hooked behind him into his belt.

He pushed her gently away to look down into her

face. Her lashes swung upward and she drew a shuddering breath, shaking the long length of her body.

"Even lady pilots seem to have feminine traits," he said, his voice steady.

"Wh-what do you mean?" Her voice wasn't steady, and she was sure her heart would never be the same.

"You still like to see how attractive you can be to strange men."

Anger, like wild fire in a mountain wind, hit her in the stomach like a fist. She tried not to strangle as she said, "I think you started this, not I."

"But you put yourself out to really enjoy it," he reminded her.

She had. Never since she could remember had she really kissed a man. Not since the pain of her first and only sexual experiment. She had shunned any such relationship, even with Chuck, who certainly held the inside track as far as friendship was concerned.

Scott's kisses awakened the sleeping desire she had smothered for years, and brought her up short to the realization she was a young woman who could still respond to lovemaking.

No, she thought. *No. Let him play with someone else's heart, not mine.* Without another word, she turned and went back into the room where music played loudly and lights blazed. For the moment, she could forget Scott and the awakening within her that he so ruthlessly exploited.

Chapter Four

The soft haze surrounding her from Scott's kiss was between her eyes and the crowd as she moved back toward the bar. Unwilling to admit he was partly right, Andy clenched her fingers into tight fists in the folds of her skirt. She needed something to hold to still the trembling, but her drink was sitting on the balcony where Scott placed it before he kissed her.

"Thought you'd decided to go home," Chuck said beside her.

Drawing in a deep breath, she smiled. "It's a beautiful night. We should be flying instead of staying here."

It was getting late, and the crowded room was thick with smoke. The bar was completely hidden by people standing around doing more talking than drinking. Jere and Fay appeared beside them.

She was tempted to ask Jere to be there to accept the cargo from Scott the next day. It would be to her benefit to stay away from a man who affected her so deeply with one kiss, and who thought she kissed everyone that way. But if she made such a request,

Jere would demand a reason. She wouldn't be running true to form, not fulfilling her promise to a customer.

She came back from her reverie to Chuck's touch on her arm. "Are you ready to leave, Andy?"

She nodded. She was definitely ready to leave.

Saying good night to everyone as they made their way outside, the four of them stood a few moments before separating.

"Remind me to go over that new tax law with you, Jere," Chuck said. "Some of the new changes will be a good break for you on the purchase of that new plane."

"I need all the breaks I can get," Jere told him as he took Fay's arm to help her into his car.

Settling back in the seat as Chuck pulled away from the parking lot, Andy closed her eyes. Immediately, Scott's face appeared and she opened them again, turning her head to look across the city.

"Tired?" Chuck asked.

"Yes, I guess I am. I hadn't really planned to work today."

She felt his glance before he spoke. "I thought you only had lessons this morning."

"Scott and Nolan Walters made a trip to Grand Junction. I didn't get back until after six." Glancing at his profile, she asked, "Where do you know Scott from?"

"I was playing golf with Jim Holden one day at the Terrence Hills Club. He said Rawlins's grandmother owned all that land at one time and he inherited it. Sold a portion of it to the developers who designed the Terrence Hills division of condominiums. Understand he still has control of a lot of that stuff over there." He turned a grin her way. "Nice to be a favorite only grandson, huh?"

"Whew! I'll say." She settled down to think that one over.

"At one time, I was planning to go after the Rawlins account, but Carla wanted Nolan Walters in on it, so I didn't pursue it."

"What did Carla have to do with it?"

"Think they were engaged at one time." Chuck frowned. "May still be, for all I know." He threw a smile at her. "She's sort of bossy, don't you think?"

"I didn't notice." *Not much I didn't,* Andy thought. *Seems to me she acted as if she owned him body and soul.*

Chuck laughed lightly. "Glad you aren't bossy, Andy."

Me, too, she agreed silently. They didn't talk anymore until they reached her apartment.

Hand in hand, they walked up the steps. "I won't come in since you're tired, Andy," he said, bending to place his cool lips on her mouth.

Her hand touched his cheek and she smiled at him. "Okay. Will you be around tomorrow? Even though I won't make it for dinner, Mother will be expecting you."

He laughed. "No, I'm going to be working on the new tax changes all day. I never get a chance to concentrate during the week."

Chuck took his accounting duties as seriously as she took her flying. To each his own. They said good night and she watched him run back down the steps, whistling as he opened his car door. She waved and turned to go inside.

Absently, she locked the door, trying to think of something that would keep Scott Rawlins from her mind. It was useless. His kiss had stirred something loose that she had bound up long ago and was not interested in reawakening. For years she had gotten along without serious involvements and she wasn't looking for them now. Besides, there was Carla.

Scott doubted her flying abilities, plus he thought she played fast and loose. *Fine,* she thought. *Let him.* Keep it that way and she'd be much better off.

It was one-thirty when she turned out her lights, standing for a moment at the bedroom window to check to see if her mountains were still there. It was quiet. No plane engines revved for testing; no ringing telephones; no yelling back and forth. Even the city traffic was far enough away to be only a distant hum.

She went to bed, lying with arms beneath her head for a few minutes. Scott's brilliant eyes taunted her and she felt his breath across her mouth. With a groan, she turned over, pulling the pillow over her head to shut him out.

Moments later, she was asleep.

SUNDAY PAPERS SPREAD around her on the floor, Andy sat cross-legged in the middle of the comfortable clutter. She had done nothing constructive during the day, after sleeping later than usual. Her cleaning chores were minimal; since there was no one in the place with her, it was easy to keep clean.

A knock on the door startled her, and she glanced

at her watch. It was only two o'clock, and Scott wasn't due out until around five.

Her mother forgot something when she sent Avery with the lasagne, she thought, smiling as she crossed the room. Like her beloved apple cobbler pie. She opened the door to face Scott.

He had been looking toward the mountains and turned as the door opened. He smiled. "I took a chance you'd be home and brought the cargo out early in case you had a date later."

There was a question in his eyes but she only nodded. Instead of her usual worn jeans, she had put on a pale-blue knit shirt and darker blue linen pants. The colors darkened her eyes and gave her washed-out blond hair more substance. The recollection of Carla's shining honey-blond hair blocked her view of Scott for a moment, but she lifted her head as she stood aside to allow him to enter the room. In her estimation, she looked good enough for Sunday visitors, even Scott.

"Is someone downstairs to help you unload the seed?" she asked.

He laughed. "There isn't that much. I can manage." He wore designer jeans that fit his slim hips and outlined his strong-muscled legs. His short-sleeved denim shirt, tucked into the jeans, was open at the throat, revealing a curling mass of dark hair.

So he did have dark hair at one time, she thought, sticking her hands behind her as a sudden desire to touch his hair brought a hot flush to her cheeks. She turned away.

"How did you know I'd be up here?" she asked.

Scott gazed over the big room and smiled as he

looked back at her. "I picked up one of your cards downstairs the other day," he said.

"Oh," she said. All of them had cards lying on Jere's desk. They were put into literature mailed for promotion purposes and to new customers. Anyone could take one. She wondered that he had taken one of hers, but then, he probably had taken one of each. Hers just happened to be in the group, her address and telephone number printed for anyone to use.

"Care to sit down a moment?" she invited out of innate courtesy. She would have preferred going outside to give herself more breathing space. Even in the big room, it seemed she was too close to Scott Rawlins—at least, for her comfort.

He was still looking the room over, walking around to look at her stereo set, stopping by the long row of bookshelves to read some of the binders. A magazine rack near the couch held nothing but aviation journals.

He turned back to look at her where she stood near the door, watching him. "Do you read all of those?" he asked, indicating the magazines.

"Most of them, whenever I have time. I carry some along when I think there'll be a waitover, and I get a lot of reading done that way." Crossing the room to the couch, she waited until he sat down before she asked, "Can I get you a cup of coffee?"

He shook his head. "No, thanks, Andy. I really wanted to apologize for last night."

Her breath suspended, she waited. He looked up at her, eyes narrowed. "I picked up your drink after you left me and tasted it. It was plain orange juice."

She laughed. "Not exactly."

"There was very little alcohol, if any."

She shook her head. "No alcohol. Honey, raw eggs and milk."

"Good Lord, what a concoction!"

"It's good for you. I have some made up. Would you like to try it?"

"I don't think so," he told her. His gaze went over her tall slimness. "With all those calories..."

She winced and finished the thought for him: *With all those calories, I should have some meat on my bones.* He had held her close enough to feel the sharpness of her hips even through the gathers of her full skirt.

Making her voice pleasantly agreeable, she said, "Yes, you'd think I'd be a little meatier. Luckily, I don't have to worry. This way I don't have to fight FAA regulations on overloads."

He grinned, eyes crinkling above his high cheekbones. "I wasn't thinking of FAA overloads."

I suppose not, she thought, sitting down on the floor a few feet from him. "I keep the regs in mind from force of habit," she said. "Anything that might add weight has to be taken into consideration."

"Will there be any question about the seeds we're taking?"

"Not as long as they come under the weight toleration. With three passengers and luggage, I can carry an extra two hundred pounds without any waivers." She leaned backward, her long fingers sinking into the deep pile of the rug. He was watching her, and she wished she had sat forward. The stretched material of her shirt only accentuated her bony chest.

As she watched, his lips tightened and he looked

away from her. "This is an unusual arrangement for one young woman, isn't it?"

She grinned. "A little big, perhaps, but I'm a big girl."

A slight smile touched his mouth, relaxing it. "Tall, not big."

"Same thing," she told him. "When I stretch out, it takes lots of room." The conversation was getting too close to her, and she was ready to change its course. Andy stood up. "Shall we take a look at the cargo? I can tell you right away if it's too much."

Scott stood up, too. "It's only one hundred and fifty pounds. Carla's agricultural foreman isn't too keen on it and they're experimenting right now."

"The weather up there," she said as they left the apartment to go downstairs. "The growing season for crops is short. How do you determine the best time for grass?"

"They won't use it until early spring. Perhaps the first thaw. It's supposedly a hearty seed that can withstand freezing even after it's in the ground."

She didn't know about any kinds of seeds and didn't pursue the question. A small pickup truck was parked near the hangar door. They walked around to the back. Six corrugated boxes were marked plainly: "Grass Seed Mixture #8. 25 lbs."

"The side door is open," she told him. "We can stack them right by the door." She pulled one of the boxes toward her, tipping it across the edge of the truck to give her leverage to lift.

"Don't do that," he said sharply. "You'll pull a muscle."

She laughed. "If I can't lift twenty-five pounds, I'm in a world of hurt around this place. Believe me, no one pampers me when it comes to pulling my own weight."

They finished the transfer in minutes. Andy pulled over a ledger to enter the transaction in the log for Jere's records.

"Did you miss your mother's dinner?" Scott asked behind her.

"Why do you ask?"

"I heard Jere sympathizing because you wouldn't get any of it."

She laughed, her teeth catching a moment at the lower lip. "Jere didn't sympathize; he was gloating. More for him."

"May I take you to dinner to make up for what you missed?" he asked.

"As a matter of fact, Avery brought me some of the lasagne, and I planned to have that tonight. There's plenty for two." She looked at him, catching his eyes going over her features with an intensity that made her breath catch.

"Is that an invitation or is it for another person?"

"It's an invitation."

"I accept," he said easily. "Although helping to unload cargo certainly deserves at least a dinner in payment."

Back upstairs, he said, "I need to wash the seed smell from my hands." She pointed to a door off from the dining area. "There's a bathroom there."

Scott went through her bedroom into the sumptuous bathroom. Andy was at the kitchen counter when he came back into the room. She was chopping and slicing ingredients for the salad.

"I take it you like lots of room around you," he said, indicating the spacious rooms.

"You're right. Lots of room where I live, where I work and up there." She pointed the knife she was using toward the ceiling.

"Your parents don't worry about you flying?"

"We all fly. Why should they worry about me?"

"Your mother flies, too?" he asked incredulously.

She rinsed her hands and dried them on a paper towel as she turned toward him. "My mother's not even fifty years old. What's so odd about her flying?"

"I'd say it's unusual for an entire family to be pilots," he said.

"We never think about it," she told him. "Would you set the table? The plates are in the china closet there. Use the smaller wineglasses on the top shelf."

The microwave buzzed and she tested the lasagne she had put in for reheating. It needed about another minute, and she hit the reset button. Bending to open the oven at the bottom, she took out a pan of French bread liberally spread with garlic butter.

When the microwave buzzed again, everything was ready and on the table. She took a bottle of Chianti from the refrigerator, handing it to Scott to open. The cork came out with no trouble.

"I can never get it right the first time," she said, pointing to the cork. "Most of the time I tear it up and everybody fusses because they have to pick little pieces of cork out of their wine."

"Are you and Chuck engaged?" he asked suddenly.

As he spoke, he was handing her a glass of wine and their fingers touched. She bit into her lip, trying to still the shakiness of her hands at the unexpected thrill passing from him through her.

"Engaged?" Andy used the question to cover her confusion. "Chuck and I?" Relaxing a bit as Scott sat across from her, she sipped the wine. "No." She stopped without going any further. Even if he wanted an explanation, there was none.

"He seemed interested."

"Are you and Carla engaged?" she responded. "She seemed interested."

His laugh was unexpected and their eyes met across the table. She grinned and both of them relaxed. "No," he said.

Further conversation was postponed as they sampled her mother's lasagne.

"I'll have to get Mrs. Timmons's recipe," he said.

"You cook?"

"Occasionally, when I get tired of eating out and Carla doesn't invite me over."

She would, Andy thought, philosophizing.

"What part of the city do you live in?" she asked.

"Northwest. The Terrence Hills section."

Oh, yes, she remembered. Chuck said he owned part of that section. Not only owns, but lives there in luxurious splendor.

"Nice," she said after swallowing some of her wine. She and Chuck had gone through one of the homes several months before, when they were just opening up. Dreamily, they had talked about furnishing a house with a king-sized bed and a stove, figuring that would be about what they could afford to put in after making mortgage payments. The buildings were unique in style and design—and extremely expensive. Nice was right, her thoughts concluded.

Together they collected their dishes and put them into the dishwasher. "I'll turn on the washer later. We can finish our wine in the living room."

Scott sprawled on the couch and she sat on the hassock, feet drawn up under her.

"I didn't finish my apology for last night," he said after a silence.

She looked at him questioningly. He turned the small wineglass around between his thumb and forefinger, staring into the liquid. "What I said about your wanting to be kissed. . ."

She stiffened. This was a subject she didn't want to discuss. The feelings that enveloped her after Scott's kiss were feelings she did not like. They had led her to the lamentable experimentation years ago, and she wasn't interested in a repeat performance.

"It's all right, Scott. No apology is necessary."

"You're wrong," he said softly. "It was far from all right, and I sincerely apologize." He placed his wineglass on the table near her and slid from the couch onto the floor by the hassock where she sat.

"I'm apologizing because I may need to do it again after this."

He reached over pulling her to the floor with him. She could have stopped him, but she didn't. Instead, she allowed him to push her backward onto the plush carpet. Not only that, but she pulled him down with her, impatient to feel his mouth on hers again.

Somewhere a warning word was spoken. Somewhere she heard a voice telling her she was treading on dangerous ground. But right then, she didn't want to hear it.

Scott's breath caught the second before their lips met, and as his mouth closed over hers, she felt, rather than heard, the moan deep in his chest. He tasted the wine on her lips, inhaled the faint cologne in her hair. His hand slid over her hipbone, down her long thigh, coming back to lie, palm down, on her flat belly.

Gone were the memories she kept around for safety's sake. Gone were the barriers she had erected between herself and Chuck. Everything faded as Scott's mouth teased until hers opened for him. The tip of his tongue thrust quickly inside, exploring, and she met it with hers, tasting, feeling its hard demand.

Warm, shifting clouds of emotion colored the room as she opened her eyes. He lifted his head to gaze down into the bottomless gray pools reflecting her thoughts. Whispering her name, Scott brushed his lips over her nose, across her high cheekbone, to her ear. His mouth open, he trailed down the long column of her throat, breathing warm kisses to the hollow exposed above her shirt.

His hand left her stomach, sliding beneath her hips to lift them as he stretched beside her. He brought her against him and she flexed her leg, bringing it up over his hip, seeking his mouth with hers once more.

Conscious of the heat inside, the need for giving

everything Scott asked, taking for her own sake, Andy answered his kisses. Long-suppressed feelings were released in the flowing warmth of his mouth on hers, his hands caressing her body pressed into the hardness of his.

Andy was unaware of her clothing coming away from her until his mouth closed over the smallness of her breast. She gasped, the electrifying sweetness arching her back into him. Her hand slid away from his shoulders, catching in the hair at the neck off his shirt that somehow had come unbuttoned.

Her breath jammed in her chest and the ceiling above her wavered as she became still inside.

"No, no," she muttered, fighting her way out of his arms. He let her go, and she rolled away from him, sitting up, clutching her blouse together. She stared, unseeing, down into his blurred features. Her body tensed to ramrod stiffness and her breath came in gulping sobs.

"Andy, stop it." Scott was holding her, shaking her. "I'm not planning to rape you." He was on his feet, his face a grim mask as he watched her. He reached to help her up, but she shook her head, her arms crossed tightly over her chest.

A moment longer he watched her, then walked to the door. "Will you be all right?" he asked. He made a move back toward her, but stopped.

Ashamed of her violent reaction, she nodded. She wanted to tell him to stay but, looking at his face, she knew better than to do that. She wanted to tell him why she fought, why she was afraid. But if she did, she'd have to think about the incident years ago that she'd rather forget.

Frozen, Andy watched him leave and listened to his footsteps on the outside stairway. Finally, the truck started and pulled away, leaving total silence.

Chapter Five

Lying in bed, her body stiff with intense dislike for what she had done, Andy tried to forget what had happened with Scott. What she did was remember.

Any twenty-eight-year-old woman should have the ability to forget one painful experience six years behind her. It was by choice that she never had any more encounters with the opposite sex. She had, right or wrong, let one bad scene set the pace over the years. After that night, she had never seen the man again, although his company was still a client of Air Service.

It wasn't disgust over the incident, but the pain she remembered. She didn't feel dirty or ravished; it had hurt terribly. Enough so that she had looked for a book in the library dealing with sex and the virgin. Some women suffered extreme pain; some never did. She was one of the unlucky who did.

She got up and went to sit by the window, staring toward the shadowy hump of the Rocky Mountains. When she was tense, sometimes after bad weather, the scene had always helped. Tonight, it didn't seem to have its usual healing powers.

The look on Scott's face as he left— She groaned aloud. He had only been kissing her, exploring her body. She had wanted him to, hadn't she?

"I'm not planning to rape you," he had said.

God, he must think I'm emotionally unstable! He would certainly have second thoughts about trusting her to pilot a plane to Montana with two friends aboard. And some precious hybrid grass seed.

It was early morning before she slept.

OUTSIDE THE DOOR of Andy's apartment, Scott hesitated. The distraught look in her eyes, almost desperate. He narrowed his eyes to look across the dimly lit area near the building where he stood. He had never seen her face with that exact expression, but he knew the feeling.

That last moment before the plane hit, when he knew with certainty he was going to crash, in enemy territory, he had known a feeling such as Andy's eyes reflected.

I don't know what I did, he muttered to himself, looking once more at the closed door. He counted the steps as he slowly went down to his car parked nearby. *I know what I wanted to do, but I don't know what it was that scared her.*

Scared her. Frightened her. It wasn't fright; it was terror. He knew the feeling well enough. From the nightmares of the war to the healing wards of hospitals, he knew terror. He swore time and again he'd never get inside another plane. But time had a way of making "never" too long, and his love of flying was slowly overcoming the bad memories.

He started the car, glancing up to see that Andy's light was still on. As he applied pressure on the gas pedal, the muscle in his leg jerked. The pain as his leg splintered was another reason for terror. It still bothered him sometimes, but not as often as when the screws and shields were first put in to hold it together.

Last month at the hospital, the therapist had all but clapped his hands when he saw how easy his moves were. One more trip this year, and he probably wouldn't have to go back for a long time. All the years of therapy on mind and body were paying off.

"Andy needs loving care," he said aloud. "I'd love to help her, but what in the world did I do to make her look that way?"

He shook his head, unable to come up with the answer.

LAWRENCE HELPED HER put the boxes of seed into the cargo area of the Cessna, placing it so that the weight was equally distributed. Andy then checked out with Jere, logging her flight plan into Great Falls.

At seven forty-five, she climbed aboard the smooth-running Cessna 421. With only three passengers and light cargo, she wouldn't have any trouble staying about eighteen thousand feet in the clear fall air. No variant weather was reported in her scheduled flight pattern.

She finished checking her instruments and turned to see Scott with Carla and Nolan coming toward the plane. Jere was with them. Admonishing her heart to behave, she swallowed her uneasiness at seeing Scott after her idiotic behavior. Carla was giving Jere her sweetness-and-light routine. Andy's mouth twisted with a wry smile, wondering if Scott had trouble with Carla freezing when he got too close.

Glad that the cockpit was apart from the passenger cabin, Andy watched in the reflector as the three people strapped themselves into the seats. Jere stuck his head in the door.

"I'll look for you to come back on Wednesday at about four, Andy."

"Right," she said, blowing him a kiss. "See you, Jere."

Dividing her attention between the instruments in front of her and Lawrence on the ground directing her, she forgot about everything else. This was what she loved most—the controls of a dependable plane and good flying weather ahead.

At eight o'clock on the nose she taxied down the runway, lifting smoothly from the field, gaining in altitude alongside the Rockies. The flight lanes she followed due north were uncluttered this early in the morning. In four hours, all good luck on her side, she'd set down in Great Falls.

With the controls set and little to do except look at the mountains below her, she pulled a map to her and studied the terrain around Great Falls. She had landed there many times, in fair weather and foul. The area around the city abounded with acres and acres of ranch land, and she found herself wondering how many acres Carla's ranch boasted. From her conversation and from her expensive appearance, probably half the county. She and Scott were a good pair if he lived in Terrence Hills and she owned a cattle ranch. Inwardly, she allowed a sigh of regret before folding the map and replacing it in the nearby rack.

"How are your nerves this morning?" Scott asked from behind her.

Andy's head swiveled, allowing her to look up at him. His eyes were hidden by dark lashes and a slight smile turned his mouth up at the corners. Her tongue licked across her dry lips, a move he didn't miss.

"I'm sorry, Scott," she said "I..." She looked to her left out the small window of the plane. Fluffy white clouds were scattered below them, some nestled into the dips of the mountains. Glancing at her hands on the controls, she wasn't surprised to see her fingers clenched into fists.

She shook her head. "I don't usually do things like that."

"It must be a special aversion to men who don't believe women should be plane pilots."

That statement quieted her insides at least. She shrugged. "That could be a part of it. I sincerely hope not."

"What else could it be?" he insisted.

Tell him, a voice prompted her. *Tell him you get cold feet when a man gets warm hands around you.*

"I suddenly remembered Carla," she lied quietly. "It didn't seem fair." Carla had been the farthest thing from her mind.

She tensed at his soft laughter. "No, Andy, you weren't thinking about Carla. For a few moments, you weren't thinking of anything but us. Admit it."

He's playing with you. Somehow, he knows you lack experience. Maybe he thinks he's the one to teach you about the facts of life. It must be funny to find a twenty-eight-year-old who doesn't know about the birds and the bees—at least, not from personal experience.

Thoughts flitted like shadows across her mind, chasing each other, trying to come up with a good response to his taunting remarks.

She drew a deep breath and eased it out again as she spoke. "You could be right, Scott, but I know when I'm playing out of my league. Give me that much credit and go play with someone else's heart. Leave mine alone."

The silence stretched between them, and she was conscious of not breathing at all. The tight band around her chest threatened to break, scattering pieces of her self-control through the plane.

When he spoke, his voice was calmly agreeable. "See you on the ground, Andy."

One thing I'll say for you, Scott. You don't insist, do you? He dismissed her like a pleasant weather report. She concentrated on the plane which didn't need any attention from her, making its way unerringly toward Great Falls, Montana.

From the Colorado state border, through the vast territory of Wyoming until she crossed its northern border into Montana, her body stayed tensed into a listening, waiting attitude. Once she stood up and walked back to talk a few minutes with her passengers, passing the time of day, commenting on the weather in Longmont and in Great Falls. It was always a safe subject.

Scott said little, watching her with an almost cold, questioning smile on his mouth. She couldn't really blame him but she would have liked to tell him she hadn't been much for teasing for several years. Not that she expected him to believe her.

Back at the controls, she checked the time, saw they were just where they should be, and a few minutes later contacted the tower at the municipal airport west of the city. It was twelve-fifteen when she logged in with the control unit and asked for a return log-out on Wednesday about noon.

"Great flight, Andy," Nolan told her, placing his arm across her shoulders. "Even Scott relaxed as soon as he saw you knew how to handle the plane."

Easing his arm from around her, Andy looked up to find Scott's eyes fastened on them, not missing Nolan's easy familiarity. For a moment, a light blazed angrily in the deep color of his eyes, then was gone.

"Thanks, Nolan," she said and turned away from Scott's hard look.

"Frank's here with the van, Scott," Carla broke in. "If the seed has been unloaded, we can get on home." She looked at Andy. "You'll stay with us at the ranch, won't you, Andy?"

Surprised at the pleasant invitation, Andy looked at Carla a moment before answering. She could stay in one of the loft rooms at the airport, which she had done many times, or she could go to a motel. The invitation to the ranch was tempting, but... She looked up to meet Scott's glance.

"I appreciate the invitation, Carla," she said, "but I've already made plans to stay in town."

Carla smiled easily, and Andy decided she was relieved. "Perhaps you could come out tomorrow for a barbecue, then. Frank can pick you up. Where can I call you?"

"Have me paged here. If I'm not right on the premises, they'll know where to get me."

Carla nodded, dismissing her from her sight and her mind, too, probably, Andy thought whimsically as she watched them load into the van. She turned to find Scott behind her.

"Why?" he asked. "Are you that afraid of me?"

"I'm not afraid of you," she denied.

"Then go stay at the ranch. It's free and a very nice place."

"I'm sure it is. Perhaps I can look it over tomorrow."

He appeared about to say something more when Carla called impatiently, "Come on, Scott. I'm tired and hungry."

He gave Andy a smile and turned away toward the van. She went inside to catch a ride into town. Great Falls was a city of sixty thousand plus, boasting nice motels and restaurants. She'd be much safer there than at the ranch.

It was crisp and cool, much more like fall than the weather they had left behind in Colorado. The air was clean, smelling of haystacks and cedar fires.

Luckily, the pickup from the shipping office was on its way into town, and she caught a ride, leaving word that she'd call them with a number where she could be reached.

The driver of the pickup dropped her near a

downtown motel, where she signed in and called Jere.

"You mean you have to stay in a motel? What kind of a deal is that?" he demanded.

"I had an invitation to the ranch, Jere," she told him.

"Then what are you doing in a motel?"

"Ever heard of privacy?" she asked mildly, wondering at the same time if she'd lost her mind, choosing an impersonal motel room over a big, prosperous ranch. Then she remembered Scott's questioning eyes on her and knew it was better this way.

Jere made some uncomplimentary remark about her fetish for privacy, and she laughed. "If you can't live without my vast experience and expertise, call me here. I may go out to the ranch for dinner tomorrow."

"That's the least you can do," he grumbled.

She called the airport control office, gave them the motel name and room number, and went out for a walk. It was three o'clock when she ate lunch, bought a magazine, and went back to the room.

An advertised movie looked somewhat interesting, and she went there to pass a couple of hours. The magazine and a paperback novel took up the balance of the long evening before she went to bed.

She hoped she'd get an invitation to the ranch. Unless she signed up for a fishing trip tomorrow, she thought she'd go loony with boredom.

THE SHRILL RING of the telephone pulled Andy away from sleep. Fumbling for the jangling instrument, she rolled over, almost falling from the bed before she realized she wasn't on her king-sized one. There was the barest amount of daylight behind the dark draperies.

Telephone calls in the night usually meant trouble—or a wrong number. Clearing her throat to keep from mumbling sleepily into the phone, she said, "Yes?"

"Andy?" The voice was unfamiliar.

"This is Andy."

"Boyce at traffic control. You awake?"

"I am now," she said. Trouble—not a wrong number.

"Sorry, but we have an emergency. Lucky someone remembered you were signed in." He took a deep breath. "Listen, Andy, you can handle a Bell 300 helicopter, can't you?"

"Yes." She waited. Helicopter flights in the dark of night were special trouble.

"Laker Memorial just called. They have a premature birth in the mountains near Monarch and need to get an incubator there."

Doing some quick calculating, Andy felt a tightening in her stomach. The mountains near Monarch were in the eight- to ten-thousand-feet range. Dangerous for helicopters. Dangerous for any flight to land.

"Where's your regular helicopter pilot?" she asked.

"In bed with the flu."

That didn't leave her much choice. "Can you have someone pick me up? I might have a problem with a taxi this time of night."

"The limo will be there in twenty minutes. Thanks,

Andy. We'll have the chopper ready to go and the incubator loaded when you get here.''

In the duffel bag she took on all flights was a pair of bright-orange coveralls. She dressed quickly, grabbing her lightweight jacket as she went out the door. This time of year in the Montana mountains, it was downright chilly early in the morning. She wasn't taking any chances.

The coffee shop was open, and she ordered two cups of coffee to go. Holding a Styrofoam cup in each hand, she pushed the door open with her hip and walked outside just as the limousine from the airport pulled up in front of the motel.

"Hi, Andy. How are you? Sorry to roust you out of a warm bed." The driver was Homer Adams, a retired rancher she had met on charter flights into Great Falls many years ago. With a start she realized it had been many years. The thought that she was getting old flitted through her mind and was gone.

"One thing about getting up early, you meet all kinds of interesting people. It's been a while since I've seen you. Still going strong, Homer?"

He laughed, a comfortable sound. She handed him the extra cup of coffee.

"Tell me what happened to give me some hours in a helicopter," she said, sipping the coffee. The air was a lot cooler than yesterday, and the hot liquid tasted good.

"Boyce said a woman near Monarch gave birth to her first child about two and a half months early. Laker got the call about midnight and was going to send an ambulance, but the husband called again and said his wife was having trouble and he was afraid for the baby.''

"Will the 300 hold the woman and the incubator?" She frowned, trying to remember the dimensions of the old-model helicopter.

"What Boyce told them to do was rig up the smallest air mattress or sleeping bag they could find for the woman. It can slide partway under the incubator and be fastened down.''

She nodded. "What's weather like around Monarch?''

Homer hesitated, sending her a quick glance. "Foggy.''

Mother wouldn't like this, Andy thought as she let the information sink in. Her little girl wandering around a nine-thousand-foot mountaintop in the fog. Her mother, a licensed pilot herself, knew and hated fog. Every pilot did.

Unbidden, Scott Rawlins's blue eyes appeared over the dash lights. "How are your nerves this morning?" She blinked his image away and thought, *Well, they* were *okay until a few minutes ago*. But fog in a helicopter? She let her breath out with a whoosh and finished her coffee.

Before they reached the airport on the west side of Great Falls, she could see the blinking lights of the helicopter, hear the uneven beat of the blades. Homer pulled the limousine up beside the white-and-orange ambulance backed up to the door. The incubator was already aboard.

"Andy.''

She turned to face Boyce, the controller who had

called her. His face was lined not so much by age as from squinting into weather all these years. She smiled at him, eye to eye. She was an inch taller than he was but he wore cowboy boots, putting him even with her.

Wind blew straight into the north–south runway, sending her shaggy hair back from her face. Boyce's thinning hair stood straight up from his head.

"Thanks, Andy. I don't know what we'd have done if someone hadn't remembered that you had signed in." He extended a clipboard for her to sign. "Take a look at that terrain map before you leave. How long since you've flown across those mountains?"

"Last year, but it was a charter flight and I didn't land. Homer said there's fog."

He nodded. "Look. This is Monarch. Do you remember the hole between those ridges just northwest of town?" At her nod, he went on. "You'll have to set down there. We hope the fog will be lighter by then." He took the clipboard back.

"The police sent a four-wheel-drive vehicle into the mountains to pick up the woman and baby. They'll be waiting for you."

Inside the helicopter, she took the detailed terrain map Boyce mentioned and studied it, memorizing the patterns. Giving the controls several checks, she saw the thumbs-up sign for takeoff and settled back. Helicopter and airplane flying had little in common, and she'd have to pay strict attention to unfamiliar instruments and unfamiliar terrain.

And I thought I might be bored, she scoffed to herself as she lifted from the runway. *Fat chance.*

Too bad it couldn't stay like this, she thought, looking at the clear outline of the mountains to her right. As slow as the helicopter was, perhaps it would be cleared by the time she got to Monarch.

If she really expected the fog to be gone, she was disappointed. Biting her lip, she watched the wispy curtain coming toward her as she flew closer to the mountain ridges northwest of town, as Boyce had instructed her. Monarch wasn't really a town; probably not even a hundred families lived there.

She concentrated, sketching the terrain in her mind, seeing the big ramshackle barn along an arroyo. She had been fishing with Chuck here once when he made a trip with her to Great Falls. One of his clients had a fishing lodge up there, and they had stayed overnight. Rugged, isolated country.

Hovering for a moment, she looked straight down and could make out blurred outlines of trees and a tiny ribbon of road. She could land there if nowhere else, she decided. Glancing over her shoulder to see that the incubator was still well restrained, she dropped slowly through the mist. The chopper motor sounded louder than usual in the stillness and closed-in feeling between mountain ridges. Monarch must sit at about four thousand feet elevation; perhaps more. It was cold now instead of merely chilly.

Then she saw it. A fire truck with flashing lights; police cars with lights whirling on the tops, ringing the open space beside the old barn.

"Hot dog!" she exclaimed. "Nothing like sensible people to have around when you need them." She set the helicopter down in a whirl of dust.

As she swung down from the chopper, a policeman ran toward her. He was grinning widely shaking his head.

"That was great. Boy, we sure are glad—" He stopped short as Andy pulled the helmet from her head, shaking back her short blond hair.

"You—you're a girl?" It was an exclamation and question all in one.

"Right," she admitted, extending her hand. "Andy Timmons."

The policeman gulped and took her hand, staring at her with disbelief. "Bob Harmon." Still holding her hand, he muttered, "Good Lord!"

"How does it look?" she asked, trying to take his mind off the fact that she was a woman. His gaze had gone from the shaggy hair down the orange-coated figure that showed no signs of female outlines.

He let go of her hand, clearing his throat. "The mother seems to be doing all right. It's the baby that has us worried."

She nodded. "The incubator's ready for it. Let's get it inside." She glanced at the small crowd of people, then looked upward as a thin ray of sunlight appeared. She smiled at him. "Even the weather's finally gonna cooperate."

The van holding the mother and baby moved closer to the helicopter, and two policemen transferred the mother, wrapped in blankets, onto the air mattress. A man in a white coat appeared, holding the baby.

The policeman turned. "Dr. Holder, Miss Timmons," he said.

The doctor's dark eyes went over her, but he made

no comment. He had seen a lot of surprises in his day and a woman helicopter pilot wasn't all that different. She smiled at him as he nodded, climbing the one step to place the baby into the incubator. He worked for a few minutes, adjusting and turning switches, before he backed from the door.

He stopped in front of her. "The survival of the baby is questionable," he said for her ears only. "She only weighs three pounds." He took an envelope from his pocket. "Give this to the doctor who receives the patients and tell them I'll call when they've had time to check them out." He looked back once at the helicopter. "How long will it take you to get them back to Great Falls?"

"It was just under two hours coming down, but I can speed up some."

"The faster the better," he said, then smiled at her. "If the baby survives, she'll have something to brag about in years to come. Rescued by a female helicopter pilot." He held out his hand. "Good luck, and thanks for coming."

She swung aboard, checked the incubator for security, smiled at the young pale-faced woman, and settled into the cockpit. Bob Harmon, the policeman, stood to the side waving her upward. She saluted, and the vehicle lifted up into the clearing fog.

Chapter Six

Breathing a thankful prayer for the thinning fog, Andy took the helicopter as high as she could, bearing away from the mountain ranges. A glance at her watch showed it was only eight-thirty.

One hour and forty-seven minutes later, she set down on the helicopter pad outside Laker Memorial, standing aside as bustling activity took care of her patients. She turned the paper from Dr. Holder over to the attending physician, called Boyce to tell him she was on her way, and lifted off the pad.

In the bright midmorning sunshine of a beautiful Tuesday, she landed the Bell 300 as if she'd flown it all her life. With a sigh of relief, she stepped down and turned into a startling flash of light. She was facing television cameras. Evidently, someone had notified the newspapers and local TV stations, and the rescue mission was being duly recorded.

"Did you have any trouble, Miss Timmons?" one man asked.

"Not really. The fog cleared by the time I was ready to leave with the patients."

"How long have you been a pilot, Miss Timmons?"

"How long have you flown helicopters?"

The questions came at her from several directions, but a lopsided sense of humor kept her from getting angry at the clamor of unfamiliar voices. The reporter nearest her was busily writing in his notebook, and she turned away. A camera went off in her face.

Boyce came toward her and she thankfully went to meet him. He took her arm, dodging the cameras and people between them and the hangar.

"You okay?" Boyce asked, pushing her inside the control room and closing the door behind them to shut out the crowd.

"Piece of cake, Boyce." She turned, her mouth opened in surprise as she faced Scott Rawlins. An angry Scott Rawlins, anger flashing in his blue eyes.

"What the hell do you think you're doing? Flying a helicopter, of all things."

"Hello, Scott," she said much more quietly than she felt. "Nice to know someone worried about me."

"Worried?" His voice was tight. "Worried? Why would I worry about you, Andy?" This was the question he'd been asking himself the past two hours as he waited for her to come back. Ever since he had asked Boyce where she was staying and found out she was off flying in the rugged mountains of Montana. In a helicopter, no less. He was out of his mind to give it a second thought. He saw her stiffen, and waited.

"Look, Scott, just because you think a woman isn't capable of doing anything besides typing or cooking your meals doesn't mean that some of us won't try it. The Space Age is no place for a narrow mind."

He was still furious. "I'm not saying you aren't good at your job but, damn it all, Andy, don't go showing off in a helicopter in a fog that looks like soup."

"Showing off?" For a moment she was too speechless to follow through on her outraged question. Taking a deep breath, she opened her mouth just as Boyce interrupted.

He was laughing. "Look, Andy, you should be used to people like Scott by now. How many times have you seen that expression on people's faces? How about that reporter you were talking to? He almost swallowed his pencil when you said you had ten years' flying experience."

He turned to Scott. "You're a businessman, Mr. Rawlins. All the time, you're seeing women moving up that have plenty up here." He tapped his head. "Besides that, we're the ones who asked her to go. She was our only available hope."

Before Scott could answer, Andy stepped close to him, her thin face lifted to look straight into the blaze of his eyes. Her voice was quiet, fury held in check as she informed him, "I have never yet set down a helicopter *anywhere, anywhere*, Scott, that the people I helped objected to my being a woman. I doubt they noticed. That's the way it is when it's life or death: you don't care who you thank as long as you're alive to thank someone."

Two pairs of angry eyes locked for a tense moment. Scott was the first to move, bending his head to place his mouth on hers. Too astonished to move, she stood there, her traitorous lips parting beneath the firmness of his. The pressure from the kiss increased for an instant, then he lifted his head to smile down at her, his eyes glinting as he looked at her mouth.

"I suppose we could call a truce. You stay on the ground where I can watch you for the rest of today, at least, and I'll try to remember that you're a big girl who can take care of herself."

With a gulp to catch her breath, she let it exhale noisily. "I had no idea anyone would worry or even know I wasn't asleep in bed."

"How was it?" he asked. His voice was quieter as his eyes went over her.

"A little scary with the fog, but no problem with the trip."

"How about the patients? I overheard you say you were worried about the baby."

"The woman seems to be all right. They aren't sure about the baby; she's very small."

"Want some coffee?" Boyce asked behind them.

Andy shook her head. "I need something solid to eat. Working makes me hungry."

"The least someone could do is buy you breakfast," he said. "I don't get off till three."

She laughed. "I can't wait that long, Boyce."

Scott's arm still circled her waist. "I'll feed you, Andy, if you can't wait until you get to the ranch. That's what I came in for—to take you back for a fancy lunch and lots of barbecue tonight."

She became aware of Scott's hand resting over her hipbone. Even through the loose-fitting coveralls, her

skin grew warm from his touch. Deep inside, a restless yearning made her feel uneasy. A day at the ranch
in Scott's company wouldn't help that feeling, she was
certain. If they called a truce, maybe . . .

"If I go to the ranch, Boyce, can we check back
sometime today to see how the patients are?"

"Sure, Andy. Thanks for the rescue."

"I forgot the 300 was that easy to handle. All I remembered about it was how awkward it is compared
to the Luscombe."

"You still flying that thing?" he asked.

"Best plane ever built, Boyce."

"Expensive toy, Andy." He leaned against a counter, looking from Scott to Andy, not missing the fact
that her hand still nestled in Scott's big one.

"It's lasted longer than my dolls, though," she
said, laughing. Boyce always asked about her Luscombe Silvaire, the plane she had bought with her
first year's salary at Air Service. It was her special pet,
not a toy. It was too enjoyable for a toy—and all hers.

As they turned to leave, he called after her, "You're
still available for emergencies, aren't you?"

She grinned back at him and nodded, following Scott
out the door toward a Cherokee Jeep parked nearby.

"How about your parents?" Scott asked, helping
her into the Jeep.

"What about them?"

"Hadn't you better call them? This is going to hit
the news even in Colorado."

"I hadn't thought about it. Yeah, I'd better let Jere
know I'm at the ranch instead of the motel." She
looked down at the bright coveralls she wore. "Can

we go back by the motel and let me change my clothes?''

He nodded, pulling away from the airport. "How does it feel to be a celebrity?"

"Not boring," she said, after a moment of thought.

"What does that mean?"

"Last night, I was wondering how to keep from being bored to death. This morning about five o'clock, I found out. The celebrity bit is questionable. I doubt it will stir up much interest. The baby will." She was quiet for a moment. "I hope she makes it. Three pounds isn't much to start out life with."

Scott's eyes left the road to rest on Andy's profile as she looked through the window opposite him. Her chin was lifted a bit as though in protest against the child's having such a meager beginning. Was she thinking about how difficult the trip had been? Did she even remember the fog that she admitted frightened her?

His eyes went back to the ribbon of concrete in front of him. He saw again the look in her eyes as she fought free of his embrace. She had been returning his kisses, but when he sought more intimacy, she froze. But it wasn't coldness he saw in her face; it was deep-down fright.

He understood being scared. Lord knows he'd been scared enough. And until recently, it seemed he'd been scared an entire lifetime. When he regained complete confidence in himself and his flying again, he wouldn't be afraid of anything anymore.

They were approaching the motel. "Do you want me to order your breakfast while you change?"

She hesitated. "Were you serious about coming in to take me out to the ranch for lunch?"

"Yes. Carla planned a light meal at about two. The barbecue is scheduled for evening."

"I'll wait to eat, then. I wouldn't want to spoil my lunch." She started into the motel. "You want to come in with me?"

For a moment, he scowled at her. Suddenly his features relaxed into a grin. "Best not,'" he said. *You better believe it's best not to,* he told himself. Neither of them might make it to Carla's for lunch if he decided to investigate the reason for Andy's sudden fight in his arms.

The grin on Scott's face got to her, and she caught her breath. Maybe it wouldn't be a good idea to have him in the room with her as she undressed, she agreed silently. She might not be as skittish as on Sunday.

"Okay. I won't be long."

She was back in fifteen minutes, dressed in jeans and a long-sleeved checked shirt.

His gaze went over her and his voice held mild astonishment as he said, "You look as though you just got up from a good night's sleep instead of a harrowing trip to the mountains in a daring rescue."

She laughed out loud, her head back, eyes half-closed. "Oh, Scott. The trip was routine." She climbed into the Cherokee as he held the door for her. As he got behind the wheel, the corners of her eyes still crinkled with her smile. "Admit it. You just think I should have stayed in bed and let some capable male handle the job."

"Maybe so," he admitted. "But you should have the decency to be upset a little."

The smile faded from her face as she stared at him. He didn't know of the empty feeling she had had when she looked down at the indistinct landscape to find a landing spot. He couldn't feel the tightness she had had in her chest as the ragged peak of the mountains loomed a few yards from the twirling rotors of the helicopter. He wouldn't have understood her long exhalation with relief as the wheels settled safely in the dust of the barnyard, or the knot in her stomach that dissolved only after she landed back in Great Falls.

"Of course I was upset," she said. "But it's better for everyone concerned if I don't *look* as though I'm scared to death." She flashed him a smile.

"Tell me, Andy, how did Boyce know to call you?"

"We've known each other for years, and I've flown up this way many times. He and I went into the Little Belt Mountains a couple of years ago to rescue a skier who had broken a leg."

"Did you fly a helicopter then?"

"Yes. A Hughes that belonged to the military. The guy we went in after was a serviceman."

Conscious of his steady gaze, she looked at him. *Funny how brave you can be with a mechanical vehicle and scared to death of a fellow human,* she thought irrelevantly. She wasn't afraid of Scott, but she was afraid of what Scott could do to her emotions; they weren't as dependable as her nerves.

"How far to the ranch?" she asked as they left the city limits.

"Thirty minutes to the house," he said. "You won't have much time to really see the place, with a late lunch and the activities Carla's planned for later."

"What else do they do out on a big ranch?"

"Ride, fish, swim. Any number of things." He glanced sideways at her. "Do you ride?"

"Not unless it has twin engines and flies at eighteen thousand feet."

"You mean you can't ride a horse?"

"I mean I never have," she said. "Am I missing something?"

He laughed. "Maybe I can give you a couple of lessons while you're out here."

"Yes, and I'll probably be so sore I can't sit to fly you back home."

They were turning into a lane that led to a big brick house, rambling back from a circular driveway. Scott pulled to the front of the house, parking almost at the door. As he came around to help her out, Carla ran down the steps.

"Where have you been? I send you to pick up a guest and you're gone four hours on an hour's trip." She looked only half as angry as she sounded, but Andy stiffened.

"I called Wellson and told him what happened. Didn't he tell you?" Scott seemed undisturbed by her suspicious questioning.

"No, he didn't. What happened?"

Scott explained, and Carla turned to look at Andy, eyes wide with astonishment. "You flew one of those helicopters to Monarch? Gosh, Andy, it's hard enough to drive up some of those roads in a car, and the forests are so thick, how did you land a helicopter without smashing into a tree?"

"The police brought the people into Monarch and all I had to do was land in a barnyard and pick them up."

Carla actually appeared impressed. "Did you call Jere?"

"No. I probably should."

"Come on in and we'll call him just in case he might hear it from someone else and worry."

The inside of the house was open and big, furnished in heavy pieces of oak that must have seen generations of the Beakins family. Andy's eyes widened as she took in the handmade rugs on the walls and the Western art pieces. She found herself wondering if oil had been discovered on the Beakins place. Between Scott and Carla, they must be worth half the mint. She shook her head, not even able to imagine such wealth.

Carla had stopped in a wide room she took to be a den or living room—or combination thereof, considering its length and width.

There's the phone, Andy. I'd better go see how lunch is coming."

Scott stood nearby, watching her, as she placed her call collect. When Jere accepted the call, she smiled as she said, "It's only me."

"Bored?" he asked sympathetically. "That's why you're wasting money calling me collect—to keep from being all alone. Serves you right, really, Andy."

"I just wanted to tell you to watch the six o'clock news tonight. Tell Avery and Mother, too," she added.

"The first big snowstorm of the season started in Great Falls and you want me to watch so I'll know the exact date to get out the ski equipment."

"I'm at Carla's ranch, Jere, if you need me. And be sure to watch the news." She hung up and turned to see Scott smiling at her.

"You mean you aren't going to tell him?"

"Smart-aleck younger brother," she said. "I'll teach him to get fresh with me." She grinned. "He'll have antsy pants from now until the news comes on wondering what really happened."

"Lunch will be in thirty minutes," Carla said, coming through the door. She was dressed in an all-black riding habit, startling in its contrast to her honey blondness. "Did you get Jere?"

"Yes. I gave him your number in case he needs to get in touch with me."

"Let's have a drink on the back porch." She gave Scott her supersweet smile. "Would you get them for us, darling?"

"Your usual, Andy?" he asked. He was remembering her health drink.

"If you have it, that will be fine. If not, the plain juice will do."

She followed Carla through a wide hallway, through a wide arch, onto a porch of brick. Heavy pieces of redwood furniture were spaced a few feet apart.

"It's lovely out here, Carla. Do you stay at the ranch all year long?"

"Oh, yes. Or at least, there's always someone here. I travel a lot and I have a condominium in Boulder."

Startled, Andy looked round to see Scott come out

the door carrying a tray with three drinks. Condominiums in Longmont, condominiums in Boulder,
ranches in Montana.

Well, I have a twenty-year-old Luscombe, she thought.

Scott and Carla traded comments about the coming
ski season, about the possibility of early snow, about
the treatment of the grass seed. Andy's thoughts went
to the tiny baby delivered to the hospital in an incubator.

Some of her cargoes over the years had been pecu-
liar, some bordering on the illegal and some downright outrageous. She grinned to herself thinking of
the three-hundred-pound pig that won first prize in a
Salt Lake City contest. The one hundred Halloween
costumes flown to Hollywood for a special party. The
New Orleans debutante who ordered so many lace
and sequined dresses it cost her a fortune in over-
weight charges. But she had never flown a three-
pound baby before today.

"What do you think, Andy?" Carla asked.

"I'm sorry, Carla. I was thinking about the baby."

"I asked, what about calling Jere and inviting him
up for the weekend?"

Uh-oh, she thought. *Fay wouldn't like that.*

"Fay, too, of course," Carla added, as though reading her mind.

She wasn't about to answer for Jere. "I don't know
what they have planned, Carla. You could call him
and ask."

"Do you have to go back before the weekend?"

"Yes. I have instruction on Saturday and a band to
fly out Saturday afternoon."

"How droll," Carla said. "What a way to spend Saturday night."

"Yes," Andy answered, deciding Carla would never believe how much she enjoyed doing those things.

Scott leaned forward. "What kind of band and where are you taking them?"

"They belong to the local symphony and they have a date to play along with a symphony in Las Vegas. They're very good, and we're hoping it will lead to some appearances for them."

"One of the best symphonies in the States plays there on the university campus," Scott said. "We've been to see the ballet as well as the opera."

She nodded. "That's the one they'll be joining." *The "in" crowd certainly gets around,* she mused.

"That's a charter flight on a weekend. Do you get double pay for that?" Scott asked.

She laughed. "Not hardly. It's my contribution to the local culture."

"You mean you do it free?" Carla sat up straight. "Then tell them to find someone else and stay here for the weekend."

Andy opened her mouth to refuse when the phone rang somewhere close by. Carla rose gracefully, her slim body something to look at in the black outfit clinging to curves in just the right places, the honey-blond hair swinging free over her shoulders.

Looking down at the drink she held in long, tanned fingers, Andy bit into her lip. The antagonism between her and Scott almost had been forgotten in the morning's excitement, but she still had butterflies in her stomach when she thought of his kisses.

"You don't date Chuck on Saturday nights?" Scott asked quietly.

She looked up, frowning. "He's going camping with a friend down near Eldora. They like to fish in those cold lakes."

"You don't like to fish?"

"No. No, I don't like to fish. I like going out on the lake in the boat, but they aren't taking women on this trip."

"Discrimination?" he inquired, and she saw that he was smiling.

"No. Drinking, swearing, letting off steam. They don't need us for that."

"Sometimes they do need you?"

"Sometimes." She wondered what conclusion he'd draw from that. If Chuck needed her, he never mentioned it. Except occasionally when he'd like to pet more heavily than usual. Even so, it wasn't often, because of her aversion to such tactics. She moved her thighs together as she remembered Scott's exploring hands and mouth, and felt instead a warmth spreading through her.

Carla came back outside, stretching her loveliness in front of them. "Ready for lunch?"

They followed her into the dining room to a round table set with fresh-fruit cups and salads, sliced cold beef and chicken, and hot bread that a man in a white chef's outfit was just slicing.

Scott poured sparkling white wine and stood behind Carla until she sat down, then pulled a chair out for Andy.

Mother would be fascinated by such goings-on, she

thought, taking a sip of her water. *She'd advise me to go look for my ballroom gown and get rid of my jeans. If this is lunch, what will the barbecue be like?*

"This is worth skipping breakfast for," she said, looking at the plate in front of her. She ate everything they gave her, and as soon as she finished, she yawned.

Scott watched Andy as she quietly sat across from him. Gray eyes roamed over the numerous bowls and platters of food on the table. She turned her wineglass around between her thumb and forefinger, sipping occasionally.

It must be dull for her, sitting at a table listening to others discuss things she probably didn't know anything about and couldn't care less, he thought. Was she thinking about Chuck and missing him? Did she protest when he went away alone for a weekend?

Carla demanded attention seven days a week from her string of attentive males. He was glad not to be included in those who paid homage to her. He had gone that route once, long ago, but if she considered him a friend, that was all he wanted.

His eyes went back to Andy as her mouth opened in a wide yawn she tried to cover with a hand that didn't move quickly enough.

"You've had a long day, Andy. Perhaps you could do with a nap?"

Carla gave her a tolerant smile. "Yes. Anyone who gets up that early deserves a nap. Come on, Andy, and I'll show you a bed where you can rest. You'll need it for the barbecue."

The bedroom was a luxurious extension of the rest

of the house. A king-sized bed sat against the long wall of a castle-sized bedroom.

"I'll call you at about five, Andy." She smiled her tolerant Carla smile, closing the door behind her as she left.

Kicking off her shoes, Andy slipped her jeans from her hips and turned the coverlet back, sliding down between soft sheets.

Has Scott ever slept in this bed, she wondered. Moving her head across the pillow, she imagined the silvery head making an indentation next to hers, and the thought pulled her muscles as tight as a string.

Andy Timmons, who had her life comfortably together, was having trouble keeping Scott Rawlins in his place.

Chapter Seven

Avery's barbecues were never like this, Andy thought. The barbecue spit was being turned by a laughing cowboy wearing jeans and a denim shirt covered by a tent-sized white apron. Long tables set up under widespread branches of tall, white-trunked aspens were covered with shrimp cocktails, lobster simmering in butter and fresh fried fish.

Scott walked up beside her and touched her arm. "Feel better?"

She hadn't seen him since she woke and wondered what had happened to him. She nodded. "I wish I hadn't eaten lunch," she told him. "Do you have these things often?"

"This is the last big outdoor feed of the year. There aren't many get-togethers once winter hits up here."

"This should last everyone until spring."

He looked around, nodding. "It will. Come on let's get a plate. That fish was caught this morning. Want to try it?"

"I've heard of fresh fish but have never had it this fresh. Yes, by all means, let's try it."

She sat on a redwood bench across the table from Scott. Nolan sat beside her, with Carla across from him.

"I heard about the helicopter rescue, Andy," Nolan was saying. "Have you really been flying ten years?"

"Actually, fifteen," she said, concentrating on the food in front of her. "I've had a license for ten years."

"I've been thinking of buying a plane to use up here," Carla said. "How about a job as private plane pilot, Andy?"

She laughed, lifting her head to look at Carla. Instead, she met Scott's gaze. *I won't take the job and endanger your sweetheart, Scott,* she wanted to tell him. Instead, she looked back at the fork she held in her hand.

"Sorry, Avery beat you to it," she said.

"I can make it worth your while," Carla insisted. "Is Avery your dad?" At her nod, she went on, "I'm sure I can offer you more than a family business can."

Her fingers clenched around the fork with which she pushed food around her plate. "No doubt," she said quietly, looking at Carla.

"Well?" Carla insisted impatiently.

"No, thanks," she said and went back to eating without looking at Scott. Her refusal would put his mind at ease.

Nolan laughed beside her. "Make the offer, Carla, and see. Everyone has a price. You might just come up with enough to entice our modern-day Amelia Earhart into taking the position."

Andy remained quiet, but she bit her tongue to keep from answering Nolan herself. She decided she didn't like the man at all.

"I think you can discuss business some other time," Scott interrupted. "Let Andy enjoy her food."

"This is the best fish I've ever eaten," she said to Carla, relieved to change the subject. "My dad makes a good barbecue, but I must admit your chef gives him lots of competition."

The conversation moved to a lighter vein, and Andy took as little part in it as she could get by with. As the sun settled behind a line of trees, several of the men brought out musical instruments.

She was listening to the music, paying no attention to a stir behind her until Scott said, "You have a phone call, Andy."

Her first thought was Boyce and another emergency. "It's Jere," he said, seeing her questioning look.

It was seven o'clock; her brother had, no doubt, seen the six o'clock news. The call confirmed it.

"Why didn't you tell me, Andy?" he asked excitedly. "Mother and Avery are beside themselves. What happened?"

"Why, Jere," she teased. "It can surely wait until tomorrow. It was just a routine flight."

He sputtered. "In a Bell 300, Andy? Nothing's routine in one of those. And in fog."

"Well, if my admitting I was scared will make you happy, you've got it. I was a bit uneasy with the fog. When I first went in, I couldn't see the ground as I came over the lowest mountain ridge. Fortunately, the barnyard had red dust in it and I could see that."

"Barnyard?" Jere's voice held awe.

"It was a big barnyard, Jere. I didn't kill a single chicken."

"Good thing. We can't afford to be sued over a chicken."

"Say, Jere, how would you and Fay like to come up to the Beakins ranch for the weekend? Carla suggested it."

"You can't stay. You have the band to take to Las Vegas."

"You and Fay. I'm not included," she said.

He hesitated. "Not this weekend, Andy. Thank Carla for the invitation." There was a muffled voice, and he said, "Here's Avery."

"Listen, Andy," her father boomed over the phone. "I know I bet you I could outmaneuver you in your Luscombe, but you don't have to show off like that."

"Sorry, Avery, but I just couldn't resist it." She laughed. "By the way, I've been offered a job up here at about double my salary. How close can you come to matching it?"

"I'll stop charging you rent on the apartment," he told her promptly.

"Good enough," she told him. "Give Mother my love. Tell her I'm behaving and not to believe half she sees on television. See you tomorrow."

She was laughing as she replaced the receiver and stood for a moment looking down at the fancy phone—an eighteenth-century design with gold trim. Her eyebrows elevated as she imagined what it must have cost. She should have listened to Carla's offer; it would have been interesting.

"What's Jere's reaction to a sister who's a celebrity?" Scott asked behind her.

Smiling, she turned to find him close to her. "Duly impressed. However, I'll still have to get my hands greasy working on the planes at Air Service."

"Your parents?" he asked.

She studied the face just inches from hers. His silver-gray hair made his complexion seem lighter than it really was, and she was aware he had a deep tan. Silver hair and bright-blue eyes combined to make him a roguishly handsome man. Carla could do a lot, lot worse. So could Andy—if she had the chance.

"Look, Scott," she said, moving a few steps away from him to help her breathing. "My parents worry about me the same as they worry about Jere—only that they know something could possibly happen to us. Not just flying, but anywhere."

"You fly more than Jere," he reminded her.

"I'm good at it," she said simply.

He took a step toward her and she stepped backward. He smiled grimly. "There's nothing like being self-confident."

"As long as you also have the ability," she said.

Carla and Nolan came in, relieving the tense atmosphere a little. Andy moved to sit on a hassock apart from the other furniture so she wouldn't be close to anyone, especially Scott.

"Was it Jere calling?" Carla asked.

"Yes. I asked about him and Fay flying up."

Carla sat up straight, alertly interested. "And?"

"They already have plans. He said to thank you for the invitation.

"Darn," Carla said. "We were going into Canada to see the autumn foliage along Lake Louise. It's spectacular about now."

"I can imagine," Andy said, keeping her voice level. She couldn't really imagine it, though, she admitted to herself. Imagine spending a weekend just flying into Canada to look at scenery.

"What time do you plan to leave Great Falls tomorrow?" she asked.

"Oh, I'm not going back. Ask Scott." Carla had lost interest in her flight, now that she knew Jere wasn't coming up.

She looked at Scott.

"I'd like to leave about noon, if that suits you, Andy," he said. "Nolan and I will be out a little while in the morning but back by ten. You're staying here tonight, aren't you?"

"I thought I'd go back if I could get a ride in," she said.

"Nonsense," Carla said shortly. "Stay here until you get ready to leave tomorrow. Surely it's more comfortable than that motel you're in."

"The motel's very comfortable," Andy told her mildly. "However, it is quite a drive back. Thanks for the invitation." She wasn't sure she was thankful; she could be just as comfortable at the motel. But she decided to be nice about it.

It was still early when she said good night and went to bed in the same big bed she had napped in.

Wondering briefly about the baby and her mother, she slept until daylight.

CARLA DIDN'T SHOW UP at breakfast, and Andy wondered if she had decided to go with Scott and Nolan, wherever they were. She ate in the breakfast nook just off the kitchen, trading flying stories with the chef from the night before. He had been a pilot during the Korean War, a few years before she was born.

"Those helicopters coming in with medics and supplies were welcome sights," he said. "But if one of them got hit..." He shook his head.

They were still sitting there with coffee and Danish pastries just out of the oven when Scott came in. He was wearing a long-sleeved white turtleneck, tucked into jeans that fit his narrow hips closely. The silvery-white hair was wind-ruffled, a heavy lock hanging over his right eye. He stopped to pour himself a cup of coffee and brushed carelessly at his forehead.

As he came toward the table where they were sitting, his eyes went over Andy. Although she still wore the same clothing from the day before, she had shampooed her hair and it lay like shiny silk against her neck and cheek. The shaggy edges gave her a mischievous look.

"You look well rested," he said, pulling out one of the small chairs to sit down. What he really wanted to do was lift her from the chair and hold her close to him. He almost dropped the cup of coffee as he realized just how much he wanted to touch Andy. His body became aware of her, too, as he recalled the feel of her against him. With an effort, he slid casually into the chair across from her.

"I am," she admitted. "It's not often I get to stay in bed so late."

"Jere's a slave driver?"

"Sort of. I have so many jobs to do around there, if I don't get started early, I never finish."

The chef, who had told her his name was Earl, stood up. "There are more hot rolls, Scott."

"Good. I'll have one." When Earl returned with a full plate, Andy took another one for herself, smiling at Scott. He never even knew what the Danish tasted like, absorbed as he was in watching her eyes change with laughter.

As Earl went back to his duties, Scott asked her, "Are you ready to leave?"

"Yes. Anytime."

"Wellson is driving us in. I'll be ready as soon as I get my luggage."

Carla came in, not too wide awake, as they were getting ready to leave, and said goodbye. Andy thanked her, relieved that they were finally on their way. Wellson, Carla's foreman, drove, and Andy sat in the back of the Cherokee.

In the motel room, she changed quickly into her coveralls and rejoined the two men, who had waited for her in the lobby. It was noon when they checked into control at the airport.

"What did you hear from the hospital?" she asked Boyce. "I saw the news this morning, and they said the baby was holding her own. Do you know what that means?"

"One of the policemen who patrol here at night came by to say the baby has a real good chance. Doing fine." He grinned. "Jere called me to find out what was really going on."

She laughed. "You mean he didn't believe me?"

"He says you're too modest—sometimes."

With raised eyebrows, she turned to look at Scott, who grinned at her in return. "Back in business," she told Boyce. "When can we log out?"

"Fifteen minutes, Andy."

Right on the button, she logged out in fifteen minutes. At twelve forty-five, she taxied down runway 21 and lifted into the bright afternoon sky.

Scott strapped himself into a seat, and they didn't attempt conversation. He took papers from a briefcase and studied them; she kept her eyes on her instruments and the line of mountains to the west. Contact with the control tower in Longmont gave her clearance to land, and she set the plane down with scarcely a bounce.

Lawrence was waiting for her, the stiff breeze blowing his coveralls back against his sturdy body, leaving his thinning hair standing straight up from his head. He waved her up to the blocks, giving the hands-up signal that she was okay.

Turning to Scott, she smiled, waiting for him to precede her out of the plane. She pulled her suitcase down, passing it to Lawrence.

"Put it in the barn for me?" she asked, receiving a grinning affirmative reply.

"That was some rescue, Andy," he said. "Bet it was the first time that old 300 had a woman at the controls."

She laughed. "Probably the last time, too."

Scott was several steps in front of her, and she didn't hurry to catch up with him. Her eyes were on his straight back and long legs striding away from her.

What a strange flight, she thought. *I should take down all this stuff for my memoirs.*

When she reached the door into the administration building, Scott was holding it open for her. He looked downright serious, as though he weren't sure they were safely on the ground.

"Relax, Scott," she said. "You're home safe and sound."

He didn't smile in return. "It was a good flight," he said. "I have no complaints."

Surprised at the serious statement, she said, "Good. Tell the management."

Jere was grinning as they got to the counter where he stood. He patted her on the head as she came around the end and said, "Home is the hero." He looked at Scott. "Everything all right, Scott?"

"Yes," he said evenly. "I'd like to schedule another flight to Grand Junction on Friday."

Jere glanced at Andy, who was looking at Scott in surprise. She had assumed he would go elsewhere for charter flights from now on—somewhere there were no women pilots.

Jere hesitated. "Andy's the only one who could take you, Scott." He was very well aware of the doubt Scott had expressed about her ability as a pilot.

"That's fine," Scott told him. "I'd like to leave at seven-thirty Friday morning, returning as late as we can, six o'clock, if possible."

"That can be arranged," Jere told him and filled out the ledger for him. "How many will be in the party?"

"I'll be alone."

Andy stared at him but he ignored her, signing the sheet Jere pushed toward him. As soon as the paperwork was finished, he asked that a taxi be called. She started to offer to drive him into town, but shrugged without doing so, going out through the side door and up the steps to her apartment.

I think we're getting on good terms, and whammo! he retreats behind the successful-businessman image. Well, at least his fear of flying with me seems to have been overcome.

She'd fly him to Grand Junction in the Silvaire, she thought. Give him a treat with old-time luxury.

She called her mother and found Avery there, too. Promising to be there for dinner that night, she hung up and went to get organized to go to work.

"BUT IF HE DOESN'T LIKE women pilots, why's he scheduling you again, Andy?" her mother asked as they sat around the big, comfortable living room at the Timmons house. It was an old house, set way back from the highway, ten miles from town. The ceilings were high in the way old houses were built. Avery had installed ceiling fans and as much insulation as the walls would hold, and it was comfortable even in the coldest weather; cool in their usually mild summers.

Andy grinned at her pretty mother, whom she resembled. Her mother's hair was no longer blond. It had turned white, with none of the yellowish tint that plagued blondes going gray.

"He's trying to rid himself of his prejudices, Mother, and I'm his token example." She leaned forward. "He seems to want to believe I *might* be capable, but he doesn't want to commit himself." She looked at Avery. "Suppose I take him to Grand Junction in the Luscombe?"

Avery nodded. "Good idea. You need to get some flying time in on that, anyway."

"Want to come along, Mother?" Andy asked.

Mrs. Timmons looked at her, then nodded. "I just might do that. I have to meet this Scott Rawlins and let him know women can do anything men can— sometimes better."

Avery groaned. "Poor Scott," he commiserated.

"Now, Andy, what about the ranch? I heard you tell Avery it was really something."

Andy nodded, launching into a description of the house and grounds. Her mother loved to decorate; chances are she'd have Avery moving furniture around the next day.

As she left for her apartment, Andy decided it hadn't been such a bad flight after all. A fragment of memory brought back the feeling of Scott's mouth on hers as he kissed her in anger at the airport.

"No matter how he does it, the effect is the same," she muttered aloud as she undressed. "Drops me out of the sky at thirty thousand feet with no parachute."

Chapter Eight

Andy's day on Thursday was spent between helping Lawrence with routine maintenance on the planes and checking out the Luscombe she planned to fly to Grand Junction. As far as she knew, hers was the only one of that type in the area. To most people, it was just an awkward, overgrown vehicle. To Andy, it was a prized possession.

Avery had had it painted for her last birthday, using the best polyurethane paint in gray and sparkling white. "Matches your eyes and your teeth," Jere told her admiringly.

"I guess that's a compliment," she said.

"I guess," he told her noncommittally. "Sounds like it."

"Deliver me from kid brothers." She raised her eyes heavenward.

Now, as she stood admiring the plane, Jere walked up beside her.

"You taking Mother along as protection against Scott?" he asked.

Her heart went still, then speeded up. She frowned

up at the plane in front of them. It hadn't been far from her mind when her mother accepted her invitation to come along for the ride.

"I'm not sure, Jere," she said slowly. "He's really an enigma, don't you think?" Her brother stared at her, and she shrugged. "I mean, he evidently doesn't trust me. He thinks a woman's place is in the home . . . I mean, now really, Jere, in this day and age, someone in Scott's walk of life surely sees women out of the ordinary scullery-maid rut."

"Maybe he's a throwback to Clark Gable and John Wayne. He wants to protect his women."

"*His* women? Ha! He wants to dominate, not protect. I can see it in his beautiful blue eyes."

He threw an arm across her shoulders, looking up at the Luscombe much the same way as Andy was doing. "When you find out what his game is, Sis, let me know. Maybe I can take lessons."

She poked him in the ribs. "I don't take lessons, Jere; I give them."

CHUCK CALLED that evening. "Hi, Andy," he said by way of greeting. "I saw you on television. You're very photogenic, you know that?"

Laughing, she said, "I didn't see any reruns, Chuck. Couldn't have been much." She dismissed the telecast. "How was the weekend fishing?"

"We didn't catch any fish, if that's what you mean. The weekend was great, rain and all."

"Rain? Oh, no," she said, horrified at the thought of a ruined weekend.

"Miller-time was twenty-four hours long." He

laughed. "And I won two dollars playing poker."

"In that case, if it was a profitable weekend, that's different."

She was smiling as she hung up. Chuck sounded chipper and in good spirits. He probably wound up with a couple of new accounts while he was at the lake. Great for business.

THE MORNING NEWS said a storm system was moving slowly eastward from the California coast, bringing cooler, moist air. She studied the radar weather map and theorized it would pose no threat to their flight to Grand Junction. The flight to Las Vegas might be rough if the system moved slowly enough to still be in that area the next day.

Turning from the weather, she smiled as she saw Avery coming in the side door, his arm around his wife. Her mother wore one of her special flight suits she had made herself: a corduroy jump suit of pale coral, highlighting her white hair, and showing her gray eyes, lighter than Andy's, off to advantage. She carried her usual tote bag of needlepoint or crocheting or embroidery—whatever she happened to be working on at the moment.

Andy stepped between them, putting an arm around each of her parents. They stopped near the desk where Jere was talking on the phone.

"Good morning."

Andy swung around, still holding on to Avery and Mrs. Timmons. "Hello, Scott." She smiled up at him, her heart missing a beat. For once he didn't look as if he was going to bite her head off.

"Mother, this is Scott Rawlins."

"Mrs. Timmons," he said. His glance went from Andy back to her mother, and he nodded. She didn't have to ask what he meant—they were look-alikes.

"Mother's going out with us, Scott. She checks up on my techniques once in a while."

His mouth tightened, and she waited for a sharp remark, but instead he said, "It surprises me to see women pilots, Mrs. Timmons, but when Andy told me you were a pilot, I was really surprised."

Her mother's smile was beatific. "Really, Scott? I was once Andy's age, you know. When Avery got his license, I decided whatever he could do, I was going to do."

"She still decides that. Except most of the time, she's ahead of me. Goaded, of course, by our daughter."

Scott's blue eyes went from one to the other, and he smiled, shaking his head. "I imagine so."

"You're on the line, Andy," Lawrence called from the door.

"Coming," she answered, turning to hug Avery and run toward the plane. "See you about eight."

Before swinging aboard, she turned to see Scott walking with her mother, his head bent against the wind from the engines. Instead of the business suit he wore the last time, he wore a tan sport coat over a light-tan shirt with dark-brown pants. Idly, she wondered how old he was. Mid-thirties, she'd guess. She turned her attention back to the controls in front of her.

A light wind came straight down runway 32, and

she took off into it, gaining altitude rapidly to get out of the way of the mountain range to the southeast. Leveling off at sixteen thousand feet, she settled back for the hour-and-a-half flight. Strapped into the passenger seats where Andy could see them in the reflector, her mother and Scott were carrying on an animated conversation.

If anyone can convince him I can handle a plane, Mother can, she thought as she watched the mountains pass beneath them and turn into lower, almost flat land. The junction of the Colorado and Gunnison rivers was below them. The bends and turns of the big bodies of water looked like a crooked line drawn with a felt-tip pen.

Getting her clearance from the tower at Walker Field, she banked to go onto the runway. Griff came toward her, his hands up with the signal to keep moving in his direction. At his signal, she stopped and cut her engines.

"Perfect landing, Andy," Mrs. Timmons said as she dropped into Scott's waiting arms. "I couldn't have done better myself."

Scott was smiling, not a trace of animosity in his face. She looked at her mother. *Boy, I should have had her along all the time. Imagine, having a chaperone at my age. A chaperone to run interference, not to protect my girlish virginity.*

As she thought of that word, she frowned. It brought back that painful memory. She really should have overcome that by now, Andy thought, her eyes on the ground as they walked into the coffee shop near the landing field. With all the great buildup sex got, she knew there must be more to it than she'd experienced. Until Scott came along, she hadn't thought much about it. It was unpleasant to think about; therefore, she left it alone. The one short interlude with Scott begged for more. That was all there was to it.

I scared him away, she thought. *Between being a plane pilot and downright ignorant when it comes to making love, I scared him away.*

Without a word, she took the cup of coffee Scott handed her, and turned to sit at a small table, paying no attention to the conversation between Scott and her mother.

"Andy?"

She looked up at her mother and blinked. "Oh, I'm sorry. I didn't hear what you said."

"Scott asked if we'd like to go out to the ski lodge with him."

"Yes, I'd like that," she said, smiling at him, seeing his blue eyes go over her face, lingering on her mouth. Her heart skipped two beats, then hammered in her throat. If a casual smile from him could affect her that way, what would a few kisses like the ones on Sunday night do to her?

He left them for a few minutes and was back, dangling car keys from his hand. "It's about ten miles to Palisade and Powderhorn is only a short distance from there."

Andy climbed into the back seat, and Scott helped Mrs. Timmons into the front. As he drove the interstate, she watched the scenery. Years ago they had all gone to the Powderhorn Ski Area, but that was before it had been developed. Palisade, a tiny village, prospered most from the seasonal influx of ski buffs.

Scott drove past the Palisade exit, turning right at a blocky arrow pointing toward Powderhorn. The narrow secondary road climbed steeply until they made a sharp turn and came upon the resort area. A sign over a chalet-type building said: "Powderhorn Lodge. Vacancy."

"Does this stay open all summer?" Andy asked, unable to remember anything about it.

"Not for business. I lease it out to private parties," Scott said.

"You own this?" Mrs. Timmons asked.

"Yes. I have a family that lives on the premises and they manage it for me, winter and summer. In another month, they'll be booked for the entire ski season."

"I read about the new slopes opened here. It's become quite popular with the Denver skiers trying to get away from the crowds." No wonder he made frequent trips here, Andy thought. Speaking of investments with financial returns!

"I need to talk to Mr. Van Dorn about the new contracts and leases. Come on in and we'll see if they plan to have lunch for any groups."

They followed him into the restaurant. It was done in the Dutch style, all cream and blue. Benches were pushed beneath long tables against one wall. Round tables with blue-and-cream tablecloths sat in the middle of the big room.

"May I help— Oh, Scott," came a voice that had a decided accent. "I wasn't expecting you until next week."

"Hello, Van Dorn. This is Mrs. Timmons and her daughter Andy, from Longmont. Andy flew us down this morning."

The man didn't bat an eye, and Andy could have kissed him. If he even thought about a woman pilot, it didn't show.

Coffee was brought out and Scott asked, "Think you could persuade Trina to fix a light lunch?"

Mr. Van Dorn said, "Of course. She has six to cook for, and three more won't be any problem. It's all family-style."

"I'd like to go up to Area Number One and look over that spot we plan to develop," he said.

"Sure. The ladies can remain here, if they like."

The two men left Andy and Mrs. Timmons in the pleasant dining room with the aroma of lunch whetting their appetites. "Scott's adorable, Andy. He seems to be reconciled to our odd vocation as pilots."

"You haven't seen some of the looks he can give when he starts thinking about flying behind a woman's skirt—or pants legs, as the case may be."

Her mother laughed. "What about the helicopter rescue. Wasn't he impressed?"

Andy snorted. "Impressed? I thought he was going to take me over his knee and spank me, he was so furious."

"How odd. Perhaps he feels sort of responsible for you."

She looked at her mother. "Why in the world would he feel responsible for me?"

"He was the one who chartered the flight," Mrs. Timmons reminded her.

Andy sat there, thoughtfully going over any characteristic that might resemble concern for her. She shook her head. "I just think Mr. Rawlins is still living in the turn of the century."

Her mother extracted a piece of netting with a design on it and began to work on it. "I suppose we live in our own little world a lot, too, Andy. Just because Avery and Jere recognize our talents, we can't expect everyone else to forget our gender."

"I suppose so, Mother." She got up to walk around the large dining room, looking at castle and river scenes from Sweden and Denmark. There was also one of the Rhine River with a candy castle sitting on the side of the mountain, mist from the river enhancing its beauty. She stood by the window, gazing out over the elevations where Scott and Van Dorn had gone.

He had once been engaged to Carla. Wonder what had happened? Whom was he seeing now? Any number of chosen beauty queens who had nothing to do but take care of his demands. She frowned.

Perhaps she was being unfair, she thought, and shrugged. Scott Rawlins didn't really care what she thought of him, fair or unfair. She turned back to kibitz over her mother's shoulder, watching nimble fingers paint pictures with yarn.

Scott and Van Dorn were back in less than an hour, and they ate the lunch Van Dorn's wife served. Hot rolls smelled of fresh yeast; bratwurst and sauerkraut were served on hot platters.

"I need a nap instead of flying back to Longmont," Mrs. Timmons said, smiling at Mrs. Van Dorn.

"You trust me, don't you, Mother?" Andy asked, tongue in cheek. "I can find my way back alone."

Scott turned to look at her, and she gave him a sweet smile. His blue eyes went darker, and he started to speak. Instead, he shook his head and turned to her mother.

"Has she ever gotten lost on the way back home, Mrs. Timmons?" he asked.

"Yes," Mrs. Timmons said quietly. "She did once."

She didn't go on and after a moment Scott prompted, "She did?"

"Yes. It was about two years ago." Andy gently nudged her mother's foot under the table, but it didn't stop her. "Avery and I had flown into Steamboat Springs for a weekend with friends. It was early fall, about this time of year. We went up to see the changing foliage." She was quiet for a moment, looking across the table at Andy. "There was a freak snowstorm and we were forced down just east of the Gore Range of mountains. Andy came after us in a Bell 300 helicopter, just like the one she used in Monarch. She found us easily enough and lifted off without any trouble, but the snow was so thick we ended up in Green Mountain Camp rather than in Longmont." She stopped, laughing a little. "She said she wasn't lost, just following the line of least resistance," Mrs. Timmons added.

Scott had been watching Mrs. Timmons as she talked, with only an occasional glance at Andy. Now he turned his full attention to her as she sipped a glass of water. She was recalling her white-knuckled hands on the controls of the helicopter as she struggled to

see enough to keep from plowing into the mountain-
side. Green Mountain Camp was a long way from
home, but she had never been so happy to see any
place where she could set down.

"Aren't you ever afraid?" he asked.

She looked at him, hearing controlled anger in his
voice. Anytime mention was made of her flying esca-
pades, he grew angry. It was becoming harder for her
to understand his aversion to flying.

"Of course I was afraid, Scott. Anyone with any
common sense at all is afraid at times."

He continued to look at her until Mrs. Timmons
laughed. "You'd never know she was afraid, though. I
was terrified."

Mrs. Van Dorn came by to offer dessert, but they
refused.

"It's really nice up here, Scott," Andy said, trying
to change the subject. "I had no idea you owned the
resort."

"Only the restaurant and a part of the land, Andy.
Not all of it." He laughed. "Rockefeller couldn't afford all of it."

Trina came by to look at the piece of netting Mrs.
Timmons was working on, and as they became engrossed, Andy moved away from the table. Through a
side door she could see the beginning of some type of
construction. Outside, she leaned against the sun-
warmed wall of the restaurant, looking over the foun-
dation of the new building.

"We need a few more cabins for skiers during the
height of the season," Scott said behind her.

Her heart skittered in sudden awareness of Scott's body near enough to touch. Her thoughts said, *Move,* but she wasn't fast enough. Scott took her into his arms and held her against his chest before she could react.

His mouth rested easily on hers until her indrawn breath parted her lips beneath his. Fingers tangled in her hair held her head immobile as his tongue inquired gently inside her mouth.

Her eyes were wide open, staring at the line of dark lashes on his cheek, so close she could almost feel them. As he continued to move his lips over the warm moistness of her mouth, her lids dropped.

Somehow her arms found their way around his neck, and she held on as Scott prolonged the kiss. She forgot where they were as her body fitted itself to Scott's, aware of his response to the kiss.

Scott was the one who stopped them. He lifted his head to look down at her, unsmiling, as his gaze went over her face so close to his.

"Andy," he whispered. "Andy?" He repeated her name, kissed her briefly on the mouth, and gently set her away from him. He jammed his hands in his pocket, turning a little toward the building.

"The construction won't be completed this year, but it will be ready for summer visitors," he said, his voice unsteady, his eyes narrowed as he looked away from her.

Scott's comment gave her a moment to collect her senses. It wasn't enough, but it served to keep her from speaking. He gave her a long look and took her arm to lead her back inside. Her mother was showing Trina a picture of the way her finished product would look.

Andy took part in the goodbyes as they were leaving, but her mind still clearly pictured Scott's face as he kissed her. She stared out the window of the car as they drove back to the airfield, glancing into the rear-view mirror once to meet the blue brilliance of Scott's eyes. He looked back at the road, and her eyes settled on the back of his head. She felt completely entranced by her feelings.

While her mother and Scott talked with one of the men outside the hangars, she checked with Griff on the weather. It was clear all the way into Longmont.

Mrs. Timmons and Scott sat quietly as she climbed back to eighteen thousand feet and leveled off. Below her, the Colorado River sparkled in the sunlight alongside the scenic highway going into Rifle. She passed over Glenwood Springs and headed north between the higher mountain elevations. Green Mountain Camp, where she had set the helicopter down, was just to her right when the light came on over the oil pressure gauge.

She watched the light flicker and come back on. Twisting the switch over the gauge, she got no response other than the steady glow. Something was wrong with her oil line.

A few minutes later when she wasn't able to adjust her secondary gauges, she turned to look at her mother. "Be sure your seat belts are fastened. I may have to go down. I'm losing oil pressure."

Her mother sat up straight, listening to Andy's calm voice. Scott stared back at her without speaking. In the pressurized cabin, it was almost too quiet.

"I'll follow the highway to Granby. If I can't get the pressure back, I'll have to go up through Grand Lake. I can't keep enough altitude to go straight across the mountains."

Keeping her eyes on the gauges as much as she could, she saw flickers; then steady red lights interchanged. She wasn't losing altitude yet, but unless there was only a malfunction of the gauges, she soon would. She and Lawrence had checked those oil lines carefully; the gauges had responded and the filters were new. She bit her lip, concentrating, and felt sweat break out across her forehead. Now was the time for Scott to see her afraid—because she was.

Looking into the mirror, Andy could see her mother sitting calmly, looking out the window. Scott was watching her. She turned to look at him and smiled. To her surprise, he winked at her, and his mouth relaxed in a smile. A warm thrill awoke in her stomach as she gazed at him a moment. Then she turned her attention back to her flying.

The gauges didn't respond, and she switched to auxiliary. She banked a little to pass over the lower elevations, down along the edge of the Arapaho Recreation Area, over Raymond, heading straight into Longmont. The red lights were still flashing on her gauge when Jere responded to her call.

"I've lost oil pressure, Jere, but auxiliary seems to be working. I'm coming in low from Raymond."

"You okay?" Jere's question was calm, checking her out.

"Okay," she responded. "No problems...yet." She smiled as she added the "yet." Jere knew what she meant. She listened to his instructions, to drop into the wind, which would help her land if she lost pressure completely.

Tasting blood, she realized she was biting hard into her lip. She glanced up to see Scott reach across to take her mother's hand.

At the first bump of the wheels, she let out her breath. One minute later, she cut the engines on the Luscombe and relaxed in her seat.

Lawrence opened the door, reaching for Mrs. Timmons. Scott stood waiting for Andy. His look took in the paleness under her tan and her chewed-up lip. He smiled, sliding his arm around her, and squeezed lightly as he handed her down to Lawrence.

"What happened, Andy?" Lawrence asked.

Jere came running toward them before she could answer. "Beautiful, Andy. Hi, Mother, how was the ride?"

Chapter Nine

"I took that filter out, Andy," Lawrence was saying. "It was all right, but the line was clogged." He studied the piece of wiring in his hand. "We checked that out so thoroughly I don't see how anything could have been in there."

They stood looking at the wiring that had caused the warning lights to show. "Call the company and tell them that new case of oil could be bad. Looks like it's got dregs in it. They'd better take a good look at it. Next time I may be where I can't sneak between mountains at a low altitude."

Scott stood aside, watching the three members of the Timmons family and their old friend. Andy was right; she was good at flying. But she could be frightened, even in an airplane. He had seen it and understood.

Scott didn't know how he felt when Andy told them about the failing oil pressure. He had gone through that many times and, like Andy, had been able to compensate for it. His puzzlement came from the fact that the threat, mild as it was, hadn't set off his usual apprehensions about flying.

Sure, he knew the reason. He still felt Andy's body close to him—her lips responding to his kiss, her long arms wrapped around him. When he released her, the only expression on her face was a dreamy smile. She hadn't been frightened, he was certain.

Before he left to go home he asked Andy if she was all right. She looked at him in surprise.

"Of course, Scott. There wasn't any danger, you know."

"Then why were you so concerned?"

She laughed. "When anything happens to the Luscombe, I get concerned." She put her hand on his arm. "No, really, Scott, I wasn't happy at all about that, but oil pressure is something we can manage if that's all that's wrong. I'm sorry it was while you were with us, but it was nice having you there."

He looked into her upturned face and asked, "Are you still flying to Las Vegas tomorrow?"

"Yes. Why?"

He shrugged. "I thought your nerves might need a rest."

"I won't be flying the Luscombe," she said.

"Something could happen to any of them, right?"

"Yes." She took a deep breath. "I could also get creamed on the highway in a car."

He nodded. "I suppose so."

She opened her mouth to tell him she knew so, but closed it again. He paid for the trip and was talking to Jere about the coming ski season when she walked away from him. He didn't want to hear about her flying.

Her mother went home with Avery and she said

good night to Jere before running up the steps to her apartment. It was good to be home, and she headed for the bathroom, stripping off clothing as she went. Chuck was coming by to take her to dinner.

SEVEN MEMBERS of the local symphony showed up at exactly ten-thirty Saturday morning for the flight to Las Vegas. Lawrence had the Cessna 421 ready for her, and she put her small overnight case into the plane.

"Andy." She turned as Jere called from the doorway. He motioned and she ran toward him. "Did Scott tell you he wanted to go along this morning?"

Jolted by the mention of Scott's name as much as by the fact that he wanted to fly with her, she stared. "What are you talking about?"

He nodded toward the parking lot and she turned to see Scott. Dressed in jeans and a plain gray cotton shirt, he strode across the asphalt strip, carrying an overnight bag.

Muttering under her breath, she waited to hear from Scott exactly what he had in mind. He grinned as he joined them. "I hope you don't mind, Andy," he said. "Jere said there'd be room for me."

"Jere looks after his financial interests, Scott," she said. "Sure, there's room. You own a resort in Las Vegas?"

"No. Why?"

"I thought that the only thing that convinced you to fly with me was to get where you had some vested interests."

He laughed. "I've decided I bring you luck, Andy,

and I wanted to make sure you got back from Las Vegas tomorrow."

"You could be right. I did have some phenomenal luck my last two trips."

"Is your mother okay?" he asked, standing directly in front of her so that she had to look up at him.

"Of course she's okay." She studied the seriousness of his expression for a moment. "I can't imagine your going to so much trouble to keep an eye on a female pilot you think should be home washing diapers."

His brows went up. "Washing diapers? How very domesticated that sounds, Andy." He laughed.

She blushed, not knowing what had made her mention anything connected with babies, especially where Scott was concerned.

"Face it," she told him. "You think that's where I belong instead of flying around up in the clouds."

"Not true, Andy," he said softly. He watched her for a moment. "I didn't really care for flying until lately. I've always preferred to drive. Since I've found a pilot like you, I've decided it's the way to go. My businesses have never been so well looked after."

"Great. I expect a bonus from all your stocks taking an upward surge."

Lawrence called her, and she went to take care of the last-minute checkout procedure before taking off. "You did check the oil gauges and filters, didn't you?" she reminded him.

"Yes, and called the supplier, too. He'll inspect the balance of that shipment and let me know if he finds anything unusual."

Her passengers were strapped in when she stepped up into the plane, and she waved to them. Scott was sitting halfway back with the director, Wyatt Stern. They were already deep in conversation.

THE TRIP WAS UNEVENTFUL, the weather picture-perfect when they set down in Las Vegas almost seven hours later. She had stopped for a few minutes to refuel in Page, Arizona, and everyone got out and stretched. Mrs. Timmons packed enough sandwiches for everyone to snack on, and they bought drinks from the snack bar at the small airport.

Leaning against the building watching the mechanic, Andy looked up to see Scott walking toward her. She straightened up and went to meet him.

"Everything all right?" he asked.

She nodded. "It's easier to refuel here than at one of the smaller fields."

"And they know you here," he said.

"How did you figure that out?"

He grinned. "The kid in the coffee shop has a crush on you. He thinks you're the next best thing to the astronauts."

She laughed. "Toby? Yes, he can't wait till he saves enough money to get his license. He's coming to Longmont to let me give him lessons."

They walked together to join the others and a few minutes later were airborne again.

"WHAT DO YOU DO while the band performs?" Scott asked.

They had secured the plane and caught the limousine into town. "Usually I take a nap until it's time for the program, then I go listen to them." She grinned at him. "It's free."

"Have you ever been to the Strip?" he asked.

She shook her head. "My money's too hard to come by to hand it over to one of those ugly little machines."

He laughed. "How about the tables?"

"No, I have no idea what to do."

"A fearless pilot, but afraid of cards and one-armed bandits," he said.

"I've told you: I'm good at flying—I just know my limitations."

"Okay, okay." He held up his hands in surrender. "How about dinner?"

"All right. You seem to know your way around. I guess I can trust you."

They stood hand in hand in front of a fluorescent billboard proclaiming the biggest, best, brightest and most beautiful of any and everything you could possibly imagine.

"Is dinner within walking distance, or must we depend on those cowboy taxi drivers?" she asked as one of the yellow vehicles sped down the street.

"It's just around a few more corners," he assured her, tucking her hand into the crook of his elbow.

Her fingers rested on the hard, sinewy muscle on the inside of his arm, and she wanted to press into it. The strength she sensed in his arm was more like that which came from daily hard work rather than running a business conglomerate. He must play a lot of golf, she decided.

She had been looking at the arm in question, long fingers curled into his palm. They changed direction in walking, and she glanced up to see they had turned into a quieter street—still brightly lit, but not as crowded as the thoroughfare they left behind them.

The building he stopped in front of was set back from the street. Almost hidden by a large palm tree was a sign that said "Palm Island Hotel."

He led her around to a side door, through a narrow entranceway, to a set of French doors. As they neared, a young lady in a white jump suit opened one side and smiled at them.

"May I help you?" Her glance took in their informal dress, but she didn't blink an eye. "Dinner for two?"

Scott's arm dropped and he caught her fingers to squeeze them as they followed the woman into the dining room. It was small, Andy thought; at least, compared to what she thought all dining rooms in Las Vegas were like. Most of her experience was in the university cafeteria.

She let Scott order, nodding when he suggested scampi.

"Where do you stay at night while you're here?" he asked as they waited.

"They have a bed reserved for me at the dormitory." She turned to look at him. "You might have to stay there, too. Aren't rooms hard to get?"

"By late Saturday night, some people have already lost all the money they can afford and go home. There's probably a vacancy here."

"You don't worry about finding a place to sleep? I

wouldn't be able to find the controls in the plane if I didn't get a few hours' sleep.''

He laughed. ''I don't worry about it.'' He leaned toward her. ''What time do you leave Vegas tomorrow?''

''I like to give the passengers time to rest and have breakfast before we leave. About eleven, usually. It's a good time as far as flights are concerned. The air lanes aren't as congested then as they are later in the afternoon.''

''Do you know all of your passengers?''

She nodded. ''They have a couple of new members, but most of them are local people. Wyatt Stern's been director of the symphony since I was a little girl.''

''A long time ago,'' he supplied for her.

She grinned. ''Yes. A long time.''

''Twenty-eight; unattached; five feet ten inches tall; weighs one hundred and twenty-five pounds; needs to gain weight.'' Scott had placed his hand on the table and was counting off the applicable descriptions on his fingers.

''Where did you come up with those features?'' she asked.

''There was an article about you on Jere's desk, and I read it.''

Her comments were interrupted as their dinner was placed on the table. She took an appreciative breath before she went on.

''I can't remember any article that was blunt enough to suggest I needed to gain weight.''

"I added that to see if you were paying attention," he said.

Looking up from the appetizing dish in front of her, she said, "I always listen, Scott. Someday you might even say something complimentary about my flying."

Their eyes met across the table. She was always surprised at the color combination of his eyes and silver hair against his tanned face. As she watched him now, the blue in his eyes darkened. He sat back against his chair to observe her more fully, his glance going from the top of her dark-blond hair to her hands, poised over her plate. They effectively hid the outline of her breasts beneath the pale-blue cotton shirt she wore tucked into jeans.

After several seconds ticked by, he grinned. "I wouldn't want you to get overconfident, Andy."

"It isn't likely around you," she admitted.

She was conscious of his eyes on her several times as they continued eating, but she looked around the dining room rather than back at him.

"More wine?" he asked.

She shook her head. "Dessert?" he went on. Again, the shake of her head.

"See? You aren't listening," he complained mildly. "I said you needed to gain weight. Dessert is definitely the way."

"Then you shouldn't have ordered so much other stuff," she told him, unimpressed by his reasoning.

As Scott paid the cashier, a portly figure in a dark tuxedo strode past her, nodding and smiling. He stopped by Scott and Andy saw them shaking hands and chatting like old friends. Then the heavier man went on into the dining room they had just left.

Scott came back toward her. "That was Harry Pinetti," he told her. "He owns the hotel." He also happens to be a friend, so I have a place to sleep tonight." He took her hand. "Let's go see how good a friend I am."

He led her through the double doors, through another set of heavy wooden doors, into a small lobby. At the desk, he asked a young man for keys and they were handed over to him with a friendly smile.

"Yes, sir, Mr. Rawlins," the young man said. "Nice to see you again."

Eyebrows raised, Andy waited for Scott to explain the familiarity. "I've been here several times," he told her. "They know a good repeat customer when they see one."

"Evidently." She laughed, walking beside him down the hallway to the elevator. He pushed the button for the third floor, and a moment later the silent doors of the elevator slid back. Pulling her along with him, Scott glanced at the key and stopped in front of Room 312–314.

"How come two numbers?" she asked.

As soon as he opened the door, she could answer her own question. It was a suite of rooms. The room they walked into was a sitting room, furnished with comfortable overstuffed chairs and a long couch. A fireplace decorated one entire wall. Ivy grew up along the bricks.

She nodded. "I'd say a rather well-thought-of friend."

Scott had walked to the connecting door and peered into the room she couldn't see. He came back to her. "You're right. I've never been this well thought of before." He grinned. "Harry wanted to impress you."

"I doubt Harry could care whether he impresses anyone or not."

"I don't know. If he takes good care of my friends, I bring more to see him." He held out his hand. "Come on and relax. It's been a long day for you."

Allowing him to lead her toward the couch, she said, "No longer for me than for you."

"But you were working, Andy. I was along for the ride—and the company." He pulled her down on the firm cushions. "We could order drinks from room service."

She shook her head. "No, thanks, the wine was enough."

Scott picked up an instrument from the coffee table and flipped it. A television set she hadn't noticed came on in the corner, and he changed channels twice before he replaced the controls.

Her eyes focused on the program. "Oh," she said. "I hadn't thought about it being televised." They were watching the concert of the symphony orchestra from the university.

Leaning forward, Andy waited for a closeup of the group from the camera crew and pointed. "There's Wyatt." The view showed the guest conductor, head tilted to one side, eyes closed as he concentrated on the melody from the orchestra.

"And Benny...Clark...Mitzi." She was excited now. If they were good enough to be on the educational television circuit, this could be a chance for the group to obtain extra bookings. More exposure like this was what they needed.

"That's one of the newer members," she said, as the camera focused on the string section. A tall young man, hair a bit longer than fashionable, stood by the harp. She frowned. "I don't think I was introduced to him."

Scott reached to capture her finger, still extended toward the television set. He laid it on his leg, using his thumb to caress the knuckles of her forefinger. She turned to look at him, only to find his gaze on their hands. Letting her eyes rest on the clasped hands, she waited a moment before trying to withdraw from his hold.

His light touch, the circling of his thumb over her palm, started a rhythm in her stomach—a thrill not unlike the feeling when she was at the controls of a new plane, testing it for the first time. Or the exhilarating feel of success when a student finally showed total confidence, having lost the uneasiness most of them had at one time. The same familiar sensations Scott was now creating inside her.

Exerting more strength to pull her hand away, Andy felt his fingers tighten. With a quietly indrawn breath, she sat back on the couch, her eyes on the television screen. If she didn't make a big thing of withdrawing her captured hand, Scott wouldn't know about the feelings inside her. He wouldn't know that her heart had begun to palpitate more rapidly than usual, that a simple thing such as holding her hand was making her think of much more complex touches.

Beside her, Scott settled back on the couch with her hand between both of his now. The tip of each finger was caressed in turn from the tip backward to the base. His forefinger moved between each of her fingers; then his fingers intertwined with hers, and he lifted her hand to his mouth. His tongue touched each fingertip, tracing along the sides back to her hand.

Her indrawn breath this time sounded loud in the room even with the television going. Her eyes widened involuntarily as she faced him. His eyes narrowed and almost closed, looking black instead of bright blue. Indirect lighting brightened the sheen of his lustrous hair.

"Andy," he said softly, pulling her toward him as he bent to place his mouth over hers. Too mesmerized by his expression to move, she fastened her eyes on his features until they blurred from being too close. She felt the gentle sweep of Scott's lashes on her cheek as his lips closed over hers.

Her free hand lifted to push him away, but even with his eyes closed, Scott sensed her move. The free hand was no longer free but a prisoner between them, caught over his heart and held there by the pressure of their bodies. Long fingers slid upward over her ribs to fasten under her arm, slowly moving around to cup her breast.

The protest she tried to make was smothered, coming out only as a gulping breath. Scott's mouth moved over hers, and his whispered entreaty penetrated the storm of emotion inside her.

"Andy." She heard the sound of her name, followed the warm, streaking progress of his caress over her breast, down over the curve of her hip. She knew when his fingers found the belt buckle, when the zipper slid soundlessly down. She was aware of the gentle push away from him as his lips whispered their way down the long line of her throat where a pulse awakened, responding with a rush that cut off her breath.

Her body coiled with familiar tightness; tensed to resist his efforts to touch her. Her instinct was to fight against giving in to the curious lethargy his caresses caused in her—it was the survival instinct.

"Scott, please," she tried to say, but his lips were back on hers, and she waited. She waited for the lightning to subside, until he would stop the easy biting over her lower lip. Until he would cease his continuous stroking of her breasts where the shirt had come unbuttoned. She waited for his seeking hands to stop wandering over the smooth flesh that covered her ribs. Before pushing him away, she wanted to see what would happen to the lifting sensation in her stomach as his fingers moved lightly across it.

Scott took advantage of her trembling body to slide one hand down, lifting her leg across his thigh. Stroking the firm flesh along the inside of her leg, he moved upward to the tight material stretched over her thin body, where he had lowered the zipper.

The quiver that his touch sent through her vibrated against him, and she strained to hear what he said. She tried to speak but his mouth fit hers exactly, taking from her the will to object, taking away from her the knowledge of the danger she knew was there.

Gone were the bad memories that heavy petting triggered; gone were the protective shields she always managed to erect in automatic self-defense. She went limp in his arms as he pushed her down into the cushions. Reaching for him to keep his arms around her, she turned a little when he sat on the floor, bending his head to find her lips once more.

Then he was forcing her mouth open, moving his lips on hers. Suddenly his lips weren't moving anymore, but were still as he slipped the tip of his tongue around the outline of her mouth. Moaning a little, Andy tried to capture his tongue with her teeth, but Scott teased her, darting into the corner of her mouth, withdrawing, darting in and out. A sharp thrill shot through her body, lifting her hips from the cushions. His hand wandered from her waist downward, pressing into her stomach, sliding inside her jeans.

His fingers moved around the tight edge of her panties, lifting the soft material, tugging. A warning signal sounded as though she were underwater, but her body ignored it, giving in to the gentle probing.

"Andy," he whispered.

She didn't know how Scott got to his feet, but when he held out his arms to her, she lifted hers to fasten them around his neck. His mouth touched hers lightly as he carried her into the bedroom.

Placing her on the spread, he said softly, "Help me." He urged her hips upward, sliding her jeans down. They caught on her boots, and he pulled the boots off along with the jeans. She was staring up at him as he sat beside her. He leaned over to place his mouth in the valley between her breasts, moving parted lips over the soft mound of flesh. She fastened both hands behind his head, holding him to her. Her lips rested against his silvery hair as, with eyes closed, she tried to absorb him into herself. She moved her hips and found his hand beneath them, sliding her panties over her long, slender legs.

He raised his head to look down at her as his hands went beneath her back, unfastening her bra, slipping it aside. As his lips rested gently on hers, seeking inside the warmth to find her tongue, she realized what was happening.

This was not what she wanted. Or perhaps she wasn't sure what she wanted anymore. The blinding moment of pain she recalled from years ago stiffened her body beneath him. She wasn't ready for that again. Not yet. Not even with Scott. As much as she yearned to know the complete possession Scott was leading her toward, and much as her body wanted to give in to his demands, she couldn't. Not yet...not just yet.

In the midst of her protest, her hands went still on his shoulders. In the unuttered denial trembling on her lips, her eyes told him she wanted him. He read it in her face, in the light of her eyes, in the soft touches of her fingers.

Scott murmured her name, taking her hand from his shoulder to place it on his belt. "I don't want to let you go, Andy," he said softly. "Can you unfasten my belt?"

Her eyes were wide, seeing dark lashes against his cheek as he moved his lips over her mouth to her chin.

"No." Her voice sounded loud and gruff because of the dryness in her throat. Her fingers clenched into his shirt front, not pushing against him, but holding on. She was drowning in the emotions fighting to surface. "No." The voice repeated over and over, "No, no, no."

"Andy, don't. Don't fight me." He was sitting on the bed staring down at her. "What's the matter?"

He caught her shoulders, pulling her up to him. He shook her, but she repeated, "No, no."

"Andy, stop it." His voice was a deep command that finally got through to her. She stared up into his face, uncomprehending, until he asked quietly, "Are you afraid of me?"

"Afraid?" she repeated. A sudden revulsion at her reaction to Scott's lovemaking sent an angry shiver through her. Anger at herself. She shook her head. "No...no, I'm not afraid of you."

"Then what is it?" She tried to pull away, but he held on to her. "Tell me what it is if you aren't afraid of me. You're a little old to go in for this type of teasing, don't you think?"

The worried entreaty of his face had turned to anger as she denied being afraid. "I didn't mean to tease. I..." She tried to explain, to justify her immature overreaction to a simple love scene. It wasn't a simple love scene. Things got complicated in a hurry as soon as Scott kissed her. As soon as he realized she responded to his touch, letting him know she wanted more.

Struggling away from Scott, she stood up, wanting only to get away from his touch, to get away from the hands that told her he wanted her and was intent on satisfying that desire. As she turned, her trembling legs refused to move and she stumbled. He caught her, his hands tight on her upper arms, holding her so that she was forced to look into angry blue eyes.

Biting hard into her lip to keep from crying out, she waited. "You want me and you let me make love to you until there's no turning back and then you say no." He was speaking through clenched teeth. "I'd be justified in not listening to your sweet protests. You know that, don't you, Andy?"

"I didn't mean . . ." Suddenly she went limp, slumping against him. Her arms went around him, holding tightly. "I know, Scott. I know I shouldn't have let you. . . . I shouldn't have kissed you like that. I know." She lay against him, her body trembling, her fingers digging into his back.

Would he understand what had made her call a halt? Could she tell him about the awful pain she hadn't been able to forget? No, Scott wouldn't understand. No man would.

His hands gentled on her arms and went around her to pull her close. He helped her dress and, taking her hand, led her back into the sitting room of the suite.

Pushing her down on the couch, he left for a moment, returning with a wet washcloth, which he used to wipe her face. His face was carefully expressionless, but his lips were pressed into a straight line of anger. He would never forgive her.

He left her, and she heard him talking on the phone. She lifted her head to see whom he had called. He said nothing but stood looking down at her until there was a knock on the door. She refused to look to see who was there until he returned to stand in front of her.

"I think you need this," he said. Room service had delivered a bottle of brandy and he handed her a shot-glassful.

She shook her head. "I can't drink that."

"You can and you will." He tilted her chin, forcing her to look up at him. "Whatever made you pull that stunt is enough to warrant a stiff drink. Now, drink it."

Scott didn't wait for her to take the glass but held it to her mouth. She swallowed obediently, choking as the fiery alcohol went down her throat.

He waited until she stopped coughing, then sat down beside her. He cradled her against his chest and they sat there until she no longer shook with the intenseness of her feelings.

"I—I think I'd better go," she said finally.

"No, we're going to stay here. You'll be more comfortable."

She tried to sit up. "No, Scott. I'd rather go to the dormitory."

"Are they expecting you?" he asked, watching her closely.

"No. I always just sign in at wherever there's an empty bed. But I'm usually with one of the band members."

"In that case, no one's looking for you, and it's too late for you to go anyway." He smiled at her. "I won't force my attentions on you."

She shook her head. "It isn't that...."

"It doesn't matter what it is, Andy, we'll stay here."

No matter what she said, he wouldn't listen. No argument she presented made any impression on him, and finally, she gave up and went to bed.

Lying there, staring into the dimness of the bedroom, she felt as though she were someone else. How could she have reacted in such a juvenile way to Scott's attentions? She had wanted him as much as he wanted her, but...

Twisting until she lay tangled in the sheets, she got up to straighten the covers. Her duffel bag with her change of clothing was in the dressing room at the symphony auditorium. Just knowing Scott was in the next room made her uneasy sleeping in the nude. Was he sleeping on the couch or the floor?

"Are you all right, Andy?" Scott's quiet voice asked from the doorway.

Forgetting she wore nothing, she straightened up to look at him. The room was dimly lit from lights outside the hotel filtering through draperies, but her nude outline was clear enough for him to see. Across the room, she heard his indrawn breath.

"Yes, I'm fine, Scott." She hesitated. "I'm really sorry."

He came into the room, watching her a moment before he walked toward her. "Can't you sleep?"

He was close, and she felt the trembling feelings start again in her thighs, wanting to reach out to him. "No. No, I was having trouble and got twisted in the sheets. You should let me sleep on the couch."

"I thought I could sleep in here with you," he said.

Her hands, clenched into fists, held onto the sheets. Trying to moisten her dry lips with an even dryer tongue, she stood there, waiting. No, she thought. No, please. She wasn't frightened of Scott. But she couldn't face him if...

He turned away from her to walk to the opposite side of the bed, reaching down to pick up the sheets, helping her spread them over the bed. When they finished, he switched on the light.

His eyes went over her slim figure. She was tall and thin, but well proportioned for being so tall. Her small breasts jutted outward from her chest, uplifted without any help from a bra. The curve of her hips was accentuated by an incredibly small waist.

His eyes narrowed, and he said roughly, "Get into bed. I won't bother you." He sat down on the edge of the bed and removed his slippers. As she stared at the back of his head, he slipped his belt out of the loops but left his jeans in place.

Hurriedly, she slipped between the cool sheets, keeping as close to the edge of the bed as possible. When Scott stretched out on the far side of the bed, there was only the sound of their breathing.

IT SEEMED HOURS that she lay stiff, unwilling to move enough to change position, afraid of disturbing Scott. Afraid of stirring up his righteous indignation again. He was right; she was much too old for teasing.

I wasn't teasing, she wanted to cry out to him. *I want you to hold me and love me but not—* She didn't realize she had made a sound until he turned and reached for her.

"Don't, Andy," he said, taking her hand to unclench the fingers that were so tight the nails cut into her palms. The lights came on, and she blinked at him as he rolled close to her. With two fingers he pushed her chin up so that she couldn't turn away from him.

"You're afraid, Andy. Admit it." He stared into her face. "The female pilot who can do anything a man can do, sometimes better, is afraid of being a woman." She didn't speak, and after a moment he went on, amazement in his voice.

"I can't believe I've found something you're afraid of, and that that something is me. You can fly a plane that has a filter problem, or an unfamiliar helicopter into a thick fog, but you're afraid of me." He laughed then, and somehow, it hurt to hear him laugh at her. "So that's it. Brave Andy hides behind her own macho ideas and is afraid of being a woman."

The brilliant blue eyes sparkled at his discovery, and she shriveled inside at the mocking twist to his mouth. *No, Scott, don't do that. No.* But she bit her tongue, remaining quiet. Yes, she was afraid.

He held her like that for a long time, laughing down into her pale face. A long forefinger ran along the white line that formed around her lips. He kissed her lightly, letting the tip of his tongue trace along the softness, and then withdrew.

Her eyes never left his face. She watched each changing expression around his mouth, the taunting smile that hurt her deep down inside. The feelings he had awakened and turned into a fiery longing were there for him to fling apart and rob of their sweetness. She let his jeering laughter turn her uncertainty into a thickening shell that would protect her when she needed it in the future.

His body shook with laughter as he pulled her close to him, holding her within the circle of his arms, against his body. He still wore his jeans but no shirt. She felt the roughness of his chest hair brushing against her smooth skin, spreading a prickling sensation from her hardened nipples down her body. She hardly dared breathe, but it didn't seem to bother Scott as she lay wrapped in his unrelenting grasp.

"Go to sleep, Andy," he murmured softly. "You don't have to be afraid of me. I'll take care of you and never tell anyone you're only afraid of one thing. Afraid of being a real woman." She could feel him shake his head. "I never would have figured that one out."

She didn't try to pull away from him but lay there, stiff and unyielding. Much later, when his even breathing told her he was asleep, she stared into the shadows of the room. When her eyes grew too tired to stay open, she let her lids drop, knowing that when she did, the tears would also fall. The tears wet the mat of hair on Scott's chest and ran over her hands, pressed flat against him as if to push him away. But he was true to his word and made no move to touch her other than to hold her protectively close. It was enough to know she had furnished him with amusement for the evening.

THERE HAD BEEN NO SOUND in the room; she hadn't noticed when Scott took his arms from around her and left. She heard nothing in the bathroom, no noise at all.

When she opened her eyes, she knew he had gone

and she was glad. Facing him in the morning would have been more than she could take. She dressed, refusing to dwell on the night before. When she stood in front of the mirror to brush her hair, she saw the note.

Andy: I've made arrangements to fly back with a friend. Thanks for the experience.

It was unsigned.

The ache in her throat made her aware of Scott every second as she caught a taxi back to the university. She sat in the lobby until Wyatt Stern appeared.

"'Morning, Andy. Everyone else is still asleep, but I was excited about last night. Great show we had, don't you think?"

"Certainly, Wyatt," she said, hoping he was too wrapped up in his own success to notice what she said.

He was. An agent had approached him to ask him to take part in their Christmas concert.

"Great." She was genuinely pleased and said as much. "The new guy playing the harp—where'd you get him?"

"He came up from Denver. Extremely talented young man named Kevin Engle."

"Yes, I watched him...." She almost said "on television," catching herself just in time.

They were still talking when the others came out. "I'm starved," one of them said.

"Go ahead and have breakfast at the cafeteria," Andy told them. "We have time."

Kevin, the new member of the group, walked over

to sit by her on the couch. "I don't want breakfast. I'll wait with Andy."

She didn't want to make conversation, still aching from her experience with Scott. "Thanks for the experience." Wouldn't he really laugh if he knew the extent of her knowledge in that field? He would laugh even harder than he had at the thought of Andy Timmons afraid of being a woman.

I'm sure I'm the only woman in the world afraid of it. Oh, yes, maybe a little wary at first. But afraid? I don't even remember if it was really that painful. Why can't I just try again? Maybe Scott . . . But there was Chuck, all these years, and she had never been able to let him get that close to her.

She had lost her chance with Scott; he would never touch her again—a woman who was still a tease, or worse yet, afraid of being a woman.

Chapter Ten

The earliest flight out of Las Vegas went to Denver, and Scott was on it. One night in a hotel room wouldn't bother him. What bothered him was Andy Timmons.

I could murder her, he seethed, staring out the window of the plane into the dark emptiness. Gradually his blood pressure dropped and he unclenched his fists. He looked at his hands, wondering if one of them could completely encircle Andy's neck.

I'll use both, he promised himself as he rode a taxi through the streets of Denver.

In the hotel room, he emptied his pockets, placing the appointment card face up. This was the trip he had waited years for; perhaps the last one to the hospital, where he had spent so much time since returning from Vietnam.

First, it was for malnutrition and malaria from his stay in the North Vietnamese prison after his plane had been shot down. Then it took months to rebuild his leg, which had been nearly destroyed in the crash.

This could be his last trip, except for periodic

checkups. And the nightmares no longer drained him of his strength. His unreasonable fear of the planes he once loved was disappearing. A lot of that, he was certain, was due to his acquaintance with Andy.

Andy. Why was she afraid of him? So afraid that she'd let him get so close and then show him how terrified she was. She was such a sweet armful. He shivered. What an understatement! If he hadn't left that room... He ached with the memory of holding her without claiming her for his own.

That young lady and I have something to settle as soon as she gets home, he muttered to himself. *I can verify that new construction contract from Grand Junction and see her before I go to the hospital. I want to tell her...* Again his thoughts faltered. *No,* he thought, *she must tell me first; tell me why I frighten her.*

He nodded with satisfaction and went to bed.

ANDY WATCHED idly as the group of musicians climbed aboard, checking to see that their instruments were secured for safety and protection. Kevin was the last one aboard. He was looking toward the sun rising into the clear sky, his glance swinging around to take in one hundred and eighty degrees of horizon.

He was older than she'd first thought, Andy mused, wondering why she cared. The group represented all ages. It was just that something about him looked young, but his eyes looked old. Turning away to see where the mechanic was, she admitted to herself that thinking about anything irrelevant was better than thinking about Scott. And that he should be on the trip with her. Instead, he was probably already on his way home in a jet on which women would react to him as women are supposed to react—according to the gospel of Scott Rawlins.

Once the passengers were strapped in, Andy settled into the cockpit and checked her controls. Two minutes later she was given the go-ahead from the tower. Taxiing down the runway, she thought of nothing else except her clearance for takeoff. When it came, she lifted the plane into the slight wind coming into the runway and headed due northeast.

Relaxing as she settled into her speed at twenty thousand feet, she kept her mind away from Scott. It required concentrated effort.

I wish it could have been different. Well, Andy, that's the understatement of the year. Her lips stretched into a self-derisive smile, bringing back the feel of Scott's mouth on hers. She sat up straight, shaking her head.

"Where are we now?"

Startled at the voice near her ear, Andy looked up. Kevin stood in the doorway that separated passengers from the pilot. There was no reason he couldn't move around, but she preferred to have her passengers stay strapped in unless they went to the bathroom.

"Twenty minutes northeast of Vegas," she said, "Over desert."

"I want to go to Vancouver, British Columbia," he said.

"I don't make international flights, but—"

"You will this time," he said sternly.

Andy looked around at him as he settled on the floor near her. In one hand he held an ominous-looking pistol pointed toward her. In the other he held a grenade.

It couldn't have been more than ten seconds before she realized Kevin meant business. Very bad business. In the mirror she saw the passengers frozen in their seats.

"I've already told them what will happen to you if they try anything," he said evenly. "Just head due north instead of east and you won't be hurt." He smiled. "I also read instruments."

"I have no clearance to be in those lanes," she said. Her heart was going like a trip-hammer, and she tried, without success, to remember if hijacking a small Cessna had been covered in her technical training. Unlikely. If it was, she forgot it in those few seconds of shock as she stared into the barrel of the pistol in Kevin's hand.

"Get clearance. Tell them there was a mistake."

"I'll have to refuel."

"How far can you go without it?" he asked, lifting the pistol to aim at her head. "Don't try anything funny unless you want to kill everybody. I really don't care."

With another desperate glance into the reflector, she reached for the map.

"I can make it into Boise."

"How big a city is that?"

She shook her head. "It's a state capital, and it's large. Over a hundred thousand, I'd guess. They'll have a big airport."

"Set it down in a smaller place," he told her. "Give me the map."

She handed it to him. Biting into her lips, she studied the airspace in front of her. Nothing but that—space. There was nothing in the air lane but a Cessna 421 with seven passengers, one with a gun and a grenade. And a scared pilot.

"Weiser has a private airfield," Kevin was saying. "You can make it that far. About fifty miles north-west of Boise."

She nodded. Fuel was not her problem at the moment. "Look, Kevin," she said. "I don't know what this is all about, but you should think of—"

"I've already thought about it," he said without expression. "Fly the plane and don't try any psycho-analysis rot with me. I've been that route. They don't know anything about the human mind. All they test are animals."

"Whatever it is you want, don't add murder to what you're doing."

"You'll be the murderer if you try anything, Andy. All I want is a flight to Vancouver without any interference from you or any other kind of authority."

Her eyes went to the mirror. Wyatt Stern leaned forward to put his hand on the arm of one of the women, who was trying not to cry.

Inside the pressurized cabin, it was quiet. Too quiet. Andy's thoughts began to collect into a semblance of order. She checked instruments automatically. Fuel. Oil. Speed. Direction. Everything was as it should be. Except one passenger.

Jere would have raised an eyebrow and said, "Well, Andy, what does the manual tell you about this one?"

Lawrence would have mumbled over his tobacco,

then slammed a huge fist into Kevin's face. But there was the grenade. What did she know about grenades? Only that they wouldn't go off as long as the pin wasn't pulled. She had no idea what a pin in a grenade looked like.

"I have to give coordinates to the field in Boise," she said.

"Go ahead," he told her. The muzzle of the pistol was awesome in size.

As she moved into the air lanes where air controllers would question her, she gave the required information, holding her breath until the clearance came through with no questions. She glanced at Kevin to see a smile touch his mouth.

"Very good" was all he said.

Silence again until she neared Weiser, a small town on the Oregon border. It had no municipal airport, and the private airfield cleared her for landing to refuel.

On the ground she gave her destination as Vancouver, British Columbia. Kevin told everyone to get off the plane and he stood in their midst, his eyes following Andy's every move. She tried to think of some way to ask for help, but he stood there, the grenade in his hand stuck beneath his shirt.

Resigned, Andy let them file silently back into the plane, Kevin climbing in behind her.

As she took off from the small field, she went back to trying to figure out who might come up with a clue to help her. James Bond? She didn't have any of his sophisticated weapons. Superman. Yeah, I need Superman to pick my little plane up and set me down on Avery's nice, safe airfield.

"How do you plan to get us down in Vancouver?" she asked.

"We're on good terms with those people. Technically, it isn't a foreign airport."

"Wrong," she told him. "To a private airplane, it's a foreign country."

She saw Kevin's uncertainty.

"Tell them you're in trouble," he said.

She saw the doubt in the way he bit into his lip. *Good,* she thought. *Go ahead and sweat; you've got lots of company.*

"I still have to have an origin and destination on file. If we're up that far, we'd better have a paper to back us."

While he was thinking that one over, she gave a quick glance at the passengers. They hadn't moved, and she hoped they stayed that way. Her eyes, moving back to her instruments, fastened on the oil gauge. A red light came on, blinked once, then came on to remain steady.

Damn that dirty oil, she thought. *That's all I need.*

"Trouble," she said briefly, reaching for the switch. The light stayed on, responding to nothing she tried.

Kevin sat up, looking over the control panel, and she felt his quick glance in her direction. "Do you have any idea what it might be?"

"We're flying higher than I usually fly, and it could be a front of freezing air causing the gauge to compensate for the thinness." She watched the gauge, then turned to look straight at him. "We've had trouble with some oil and filters lately. I imagine this is some of that trouble. My advice is for you to strap yourself into the seat until I figure out what to do about this. There's nowhere for us to land out here, I can tell you that."

"Try to raise someone," he ordered.

"We're too far south of Pendleton and we're in the middle of the Blue Mountains." She tried the radio, but there was nothing but static.

"Keep trying," he said. "I'm going to strap myself in, but I don't have to remind you, your passengers are there with me."

She nodded. Turning her hand over, she saw the palm was wet. She wiped it on the coveralls she had pulled on over her jeans before leaving Las Vegas. Passing the back of her hand across her mouth, she felt the moisture on her upper lip. Her eyes went back to the lighted oil gauge.

If I live, I'll sue that oil company, she thought. Her eyes narrowed. The oil gauge. Well, now... Her left hand couldn't be seen from the passenger area. The mirror showed Kevin strapped into a seat, half facing the other passengers. Wyatt Stern watched Kevin, his expression impassive.

The fingers of her left hand fiddled with the controls, leaving the oil gauge loose as she twisted. She cut the motor, switching it back on immediately. There was a stutter of the engines before they recaught, and lights came on all across the control board.

"What happened?" Kevin asked, his voice loud and tight. He was becoming extremely nervous.

Not too nervous, she begged silently. *Don't let his trigger hand get too unsteady.*

"The fuel line may be choked, too, besides the oil," she said. "We're losing altitude." The plane dropped downward, and she could almost feel the indrawn breaths.

Mountain peaks came up at them at an alarming speed, and she eased up on her downdraft. Pendleton had a municipal airport, she had noticed as they looked at the map. They were several miles below Pendleton and she could remember nothing else on the map. Nothing except a highway. *Sunday afternoon traffic,* she thought. *I certainly can pick my times.*

"I'm going to try to land on that road down there," she told them in a voice as steady as she could make it. "That's our only chance." She watched Kevin in the mirror. His eyes bore into the back of her head as he tried to decide if she was doing all she could. The fact that she was landing on a road instead of at an airport seemed to convince him she had no choice.

"I'm going to try the radio, Kevin. We'd better let someone know in case we don't make it down in one piece."

"Go ahead." He was shaking his head as he went on, "Of all the crazy people I have to pick to take me to Vancouver, it's a female pilot with plane trouble." He gave a half-grin, meeting her eyes in the reflector.

A moment later, a voice came through the earphones. "T520 to pilot. Come in."

Breathing a tiny prayer, Andy answered. "CT64-26NA. Going down vicinity highway south of Pendleton. Eight people aboard. Losing power."

"C421, give coordinates. Over."

She read them off quickly, adding, "We have a—"

"Shut up," Kevin said. "That's enough."

He guessed her intention of telling she was under pressure other than a forced landing. He had left the seat and now reached to turn the switch, cutting off their contact.

She swallowed. "You'd better sit down, Kevin," she said. After a moment she felt, rather than saw, that he went back to sit with the other passengers. She didn't look to see what else he did—she was too busy.

The road came up to meet them. A hasty glance showed it empty. Not even a cow or a deer. They hit hard and the impact shook the plane, whirling it around and tilting it crazily for an instant before it settled back with a teeth-rattling bounce.

Oh, Lord, that grenade, she thought as she heard the noise, recognizing it as a blown tire. She sat only for an instant, stunned, before she left the controls and ran back to the passengers."

"Get out of here," she ordered. "There could be a fire. Move it. You, too, Kevin." He was standing uncertainly, still with the gun pointed, the grenade grasped in his fist. He was behind her as the last of the passengers scrambled out.

They faced each other. "Whatever you do, it had better be fast. If the gas and oil both are leaking...." She let the sentence drop, looking him straight in the eye.

"Get out," he said.

Hesitating only a moment, she swung down and walked quickly away to join the others. When she turned, Kevin was running across the road toward the mountains in the distance.

"Kevin, wait," she called, but he paid no attention. They watched him disappear out of sight without speaking. In the quiet of the Sunday afternoon, sirens sounded in the direction of Pendleton.

Taking a deep breath, she turned to face her passengers. Before she could speak, Wyatt stepped forward.

"On behalf of all of us, thanks," he said.

Her eyes went over the group. Three men and two women, along with their director, on a routine date to play with the symphony in Las Vegas. It was a sea of white faces.

Andy grinned. "You're welcome." She was suddenly caught up in their arms and squeezed breathless.

The sirens came closer, and they turned as one to see ambulance and police cars converging on them. For the first time, she looked at her plane.

Smoke came from the ruptured tire. The fiberglass wing tip on the left was rather scrunched-looking where it had taken some of the asphalt from the road. It had come through like the champion it was.

There was a loud blast of a horn, and they turned to see a sixteen-wheeler semitrailer pull up close to the plane blocking the road. The driver climbed down and stood scratching his head, looking at the plane.

"Well," Wyatt said, "I'll bet he'll have trouble explaining to his boss that he's late because a plane got in his way."

"The first thing we'd better do is call home and let them know where we are," she said to the policeman who was filling out the report. He nodded, pointing to a telephone. As she went to place the call, he continued to question her passengers about Kevin and what they knew about him.

Nothing much was known. He had joined the symphony only a few weeks before, coming with high recommendations from someone Wyatt knew in Denver. That was all.

JERE HAD ARRIVED at the airfield only a few minutes before Andy called. He had come because Andy's plane was due to land within the hour, and he and Lawrence were to take care of the plane.

"Ever been to Pendleton, Oregon, Jere?" Andy asked by way of opening the conversation.

"Pendleton? Nope, can't say that I have. What are you doing calling home? You're due here in twenty minutes."

"I'm gonna be a little late, Jere. Would you apologize to Mother for me? I'm afraid I'll miss dinner, too."

There was a silence on the other end of the line. She waited.

"What happened, Andy? Are you okay?"

"Got a minute? It's quite a story."

Chapter Eleven

They spent the night in a motel in Pendleton. Wyatt and his musicians discussed over and over the traumatic experience at the hands of one of their own members.

"What do you suppose made him do anything like that, Andy?" Wyatt asked her.

"I suppose a psychiatrist would say he's sick or mentally disturbed. I don't know, Wyatt." She watched the older man as they drank coffee one of them had brought from the motel dining room. She hadn't been able to eat; her stomach was still churning.

The police and National Guardsmen were searching for Kevin in the hills and mountains, but as darkness fell, no one had seen any sign of him.

Her plane was left at the airfield. Avery and Lawrence would fly in Monday and see how long repairs would take before it could be flown. Andy planned to fly the Cessna 414 that Avery and Lawrence came in back to Longmont with her passengers.

"You won't be afraid to get right back into a plane,

Andy?'' Johnny, the cellist in the group, asked.

"Not as long as no one's carrying a grenade or a pistol," she told him.

"What about the trouble you had?" someone else asked.

"Sorry. I had to make it really look bad to get his attention. The oil gauge was only a warning; we could have made it to another airfield easily enough."

Sharing a room with the two girls in the band, Andy lay awake long after they stopped talking about the trip. The string-taut tightness of her body refused to let her relax, and she stared toward the ceiling of the room. Lights from passing cars faded in and out as the hours passed.

It could have been a tragedy. God only knew why it hadn't been. Only He knew why the grenade didn't explode. Well, perhaps Kevin Engle knew. Only Kevin knew why he had started the charade. Not really a charade. He had told her what he wanted, not why—just that he wanted to go to Vancouver.

Andy'd always wanted to go to Vancouver. She remembered hoping that maybe one day Chuck would invite her to go along on one of his fishing expeditions up that way.

And against all reasoning, Scott intruded in her thoughts. Suppose she'd been killed? Would he still think she was never frightened? Only of him? It was close, Scott, she wanted to tell him. *I came very close to overcoming my fear of you—or of being a woman—or whatever it was that sent me into panic. I also came very close to not being able to tell you again how sorry I am for what happened.* She twisted. Nerves in her legs jerked, and she sat up to rub the tense calves with her balled-up fist.

Finally, when she lay down again, she remembered the feel of Scott's body against hers, still in jeans. Her fingers curled as she recalled the wiry chest hairs that were wet when she went to sleep in the early-morning hours.

Scott. She buried her face in the pillow, sleeping restlessly until daylight.

"HI, AVERY," she said. Her dad strode toward her, Lawrence right behind him. He stopped in front of her, looking straight into his daughter's eyes.

"You okay?" he asked quietly.

Andy nodded and was caught up in long arms, squeezing her tightly. Over his thick shoulder, she winked at Lawrence, who reached up to take her hand as she patted Avery's back.

They all talked at once. Wyatt's group stood to one side, watching Andy's reunion with her family. When everything had been described and gone over several times, Andy looked at Avery.

"Mother worried?" she asked.

"Well, she didn't worry too much about it until this morning, when she happened to think about the oil gauge problem you had the other day. She got sort of upet when she realized that was too much of a coincidence."

He shook his head. "Last night about midnight, I called the president of the company that made that shipment. After he got over being upset at being awakened at that time and found out what I called about, he decided to make a trip out here himself to investigate." He grinned at her. "I thought he might see it my way."

"Go ahead and load up, Wyatt," she told him. "I want to look over the plane with Dad and Lawrence." The plane had been brought in from the crash landing site by one of the mechanics at the field.

The three of them stood there, looking at the damage to her plane. It was slight by crash standards. A blown tire, ripped wing tip and a piece of loose metal.

Lawrence went over it with meticulous care and came back to stand in front of her and Avery. He spit into the dust at their feet.

"You carry a rabbit's foot, Andy?" he inquired.

"The one you gave me when I turned sixteen," she told him.

He nodded, walking back to swing up into the plane. She met her dad's smiling glance.

"You don't need me, do you, Lawrence?" she called.

At his muffled negative reply, she hugged Avery. "See you tomorrow, I guess?"

"Yes. Tell Mother not to worry."

She nodded and, turning, ran across the field to the smaller Cessna waiting for her. They made a stop to refuel at Rock Springs in Wyoming and made it home without further incident.

At five o'clock, she yelled at Stuart, one of the mechanics, "Put it in the barn for me?"

Wyatt led his group inside the administrative building to call a van to pick them up. Jere leaned casually against the counter as Andy joined them.

"Honestly, Andy, you can't be trusted out of my sight." He sighed loudly. "You go chasing up a foggy mountain in a helicopter in Montana. Send you on a perfectly routine flight to Las Vegas and you get hijacked." He shook his head, eyeing his sister as she rounded the counter. "Do you know the odds of getting hijacked in a Cessna 421? About one in eight hundred and forty thousand, according to the Bureau of Statistics."

She stopped near him and shrugged. "If not for me, this place would be completely without excitement." Jere reached out, gathering her to him in a bear hug.

A FEW HOURS LATER, Andy sat slumped against her mother's chair, wrapped in a terry robe. The phone hadn't stopped ringing. Newspapers called; television reporters from as far away as Denver called. There was still no word on Kevin Engle. No one could come up with a plausible explanation why he had pulled the hijack to Vancouver. No one knew what had happened to him.

"What will they do if they catch him, Jere?" she asked. So tired she couldn't sit still, she worried about Kevin out there in the rugged mountains. It turned cold this time of year, and he had only a thin sweater when he left the plane.

"It's a federal offense, Andy," he said. "Even a private plane is covered by hijacking regulations because of air-lane regs."

"Guess they didn't find him or Dad would have called," she said. Her brother nodded.

A few minutes later, Jere and Fay left, admitting the phone was driving them crazy. Mrs. Timmons hooked up the telephone recorder, and there was blessed silence.

Andy stood up and looked at her mother. "Thanks for the invitation to stay overnight. I don't think I'd have made it upstairs." Waving good night, she went down the hall to the room that had been hers ever since she could remember. Her body ached as she slid between the light blankets. In the crash landing, her ribs had been forced against a metal panel, and she was sore and stiff.

I wish Scott were here to hold me, she thought. *At least I'd have a good excuse for him not to make love to me. I'm too sore.* He probably wouldn't give me another chance to make an excuse, she decided, and numb with exhaustion, she fell asleep.

"Do you want to talk to any more people from the newspapers, Andy?" her mother asked.

It was Tuesday morning, a cool, rainy morning in early October. Andy sat in the breakfast nook, staring out at the dripping leaves that had gone from green to yellow and orange in the short time between her trip to Great Falls and the misadventure to Las Vegas. The air was not only wet but also had a definite fall chill in it.

"I've told them everything I know, Mother. Why can't they leave it alone? I can't add even one new punctuation mark to the story. Kevin is the only one that can shed any more light, and until they find him, I'd just as soon forget it.''

Mrs. Timmons gave her a sympathetic smile and nodded. ''Have you heard from Scott?''

Her fingers tightened around her coffee cup as she shook her head. ''I'm just glad he came back early. Perhaps he had a premonition.'' A premonition wasn't what he had. An enlightening was more to the point.

She thought perhaps he'd call to let them know he was thinking about her, but so far, no word. The incident had been reported everywhere; there was no way he couldn't have heard about it. *Another experience, Scott, that won't give me the help I need.*

Avery called from Pendleton, telling her the plane could be repaired by Wednesday. ''Stay home and rest, Andy,'' he added before he hung up.

She was too restless to stay still. As she stood up, she winced. Every time she moved, she found a new sore place.

''Perhaps you should go to the doctor, Andy, and get something for all your bruises. Let him take X rays to see if there are any broken bones.''

''No broken bones, Mother, or I couldn't move at all. I'll be all right as soon as I get home and soak for a few hours in the tub.''

The coolness of the rain felt good as she took her time getting into her car. She waved to her mother, who stood in the doorway watching her leave. As she parked near the administration building, she looked across the field to the hangar where she usually saw Lawrence working on the Cessna 421. A shiver of downright terror went through her as she thought of what *could* have happened.

Jere was on the phone. From his facial expression and the way he widened his eyes at her, she assumed it was reporters or someone curious about the reported hijacking of the small plane.

Insurance papers were lying on the counter, and she stopped a moment to look at what Jere had written. Under "injuries," he had written "minor." Thankfully, no one even had a scratch. Except for her sore ribs.

Lucky, lucky, she thought. As Jere hung up the phone she faced him, able to smile this morning. The night before she hadn't been able to muster even a weak one.

"No flights today?" she asked hopefully.

He grinned. "No flights. By the time you get through talking to everyone who calls, however, you may wish you were back in Las Vegas."

"No, thanks. I'll face my doubtful public," she said, her voice dry. Las Vegas did not have very good memories for her at the moment.

"Insurance adjusters will be out as soon as Avery gets the plane back. I think the guy was ready to hug your neck when I said no injuries." When she only nodded and didn't say anything, he went on, "How Andy? How'd you get it down on that road losing oil pressure and misfiring?"

She shook her head, eyeing him sadly. "My own brother has doubts about my ability. I can't believe it."

"Listen, Andy, my love. With your shenanigans of

the last week or so, I'm beginning to believe anything."

She laughed, and his expression changed from concern to a friendly grin. "What about Scott?"

Stiffening at the unexpected question, she stared at him a moment before turning away. "He made out all right, I'd say, since he chose to return early."

"I mean, has he called?" Jere insisted.

"No." She frowned as she said, "You know, I really thought he would. Surely he heard about it." It was an effort, but she made her voice sound teasing as she went on. "Maybe he went into shock when he heard what happened. It was a close call for him."

Not nearly as close as the call I had—and that's not even talking about the accident. Her thoughts ran amok down the line she tried to keep away from. A charge of excitement ran through her, electricity at the remembered touch of Scott's hands on her, an awareness of her body in a way she had never known before his kisses.

We came so close, so very close. Inwardly she groaned, but looking at Jere, she said only, "Perhaps he tried to call, but the phones have been so busy, he couldn't get through." She knew it wasn't true, but it was as good an excuse for her weary heart as any. "Whatever the case, I'm going home and take a two-hour hot bath. Don't call me, Jere, I'll call you." She walked around the counter. "Next week."

Behind her, she heard his laugh as she swung through the wide doorway and up the stairs to her apartment.

"Beautiful," she said aloud as she stood inside her

door, looking around at the spacious room. Sunday morning was a long, long time ago.

It wasn't quite two hours later when she emerged from the steamy bathroom, wrapped in a thirsty terry-cloth towel. She stood for a few minutes in front of the dressing table drying her hair. There was a slight scratch near the curve of her jaw she hadn't noticed until then. Taking a moisturizer, she spread it liberally over her face and over the abrasion.

In the bedroom again, she looked at the big bed. Sure looks comfortable, she mused. Dropping the towel on the floor, she turned back the covers and slid between the sheets. "Ah-hh-h," she sighed.

Sometime later she heard the doorbell ring through her sleep-drugged consciousness. Struggling to open her eyes and sit up, she looked at her watch and blinked. It was four o'clock.

The chimes from the door echoed through her fogginess, and she fought with the sheets to get out of bed.

"A minute. Just a minute," she called but the bell kept on ringing.

Muttering uncomplimentary things at Jere, she grabbed a robe and half ran to the door. Jerking the door wide, she opened her mouth to tell her brother to lay off the noise.

Scott was leaning against the balcony railing, looking across toward the Rocky Mountains. Completely nonplussed, she stared at him, blinking in the watery sunlight that had decided to come through.

"Oh!" was the most she could manage. She gulped and moved back into the room.

Before he turned from the balcony, his eyes went over her, taking in her tousled hair, eyes still sleep filled, bare feet beneath the robe carelessly thrown around her. His once-over completed, he walked past her into the room.

Leaning against the door after she closed it, she waited for him to speak. His appearance had robbed her of any thought or ability to say even hello.

"Are you going to stand there and not say anything? Or do you think we might sit down and talk?" he asked.

His hands were shoved into the tan Windbreaker he wore. His bright silver hair was windblown out of its usual neat style. The odd darkness of his eyelashes contrasted with his hair and with the bright blue of his eyes.

Fighting the sudden desire to fly into his arms, she walked around him toward the kitchen. She shoved her own hands deep into the robe pockets.

"Good morning, Scott," she said. "Would you like some coffee?"

"It's afternoon, Andy," he reminded her. "No, I don't want coffee. I want to ask you a few questions."

In midstride, she turned away from the kitchen and back to the couch in the living room. He followed her, waiting until she dropped onto the thick cushions of the couch before he sat in front of her in the big chair.

He leaned toward her, his glance traveling over her face. "I didn't get into town until about noon today. I didn't know about the incident until Nolan told me." He continued to watch her.

Andy nodded but didn't say anything. Her ability to

speak was still too uncertain for her to risk it. Her body felt sluggish and uncoordinated, and her tongue felt stuck to the roof of a very dry mouth.

He hesitated as she remained silent. "I suppose you've talked about it so much you'd rather not say anything?"

Clearing her throat and swallowing, she sat up straighter on the couch. Her fingers rubbed along the piping on the cushions.

"It—it..." She lifted her head to look directly into his eyes for the first time. "I'm glad you left early, Scott. I guess—I suppose..." Starting over, she went on, "It was the luckiest part of the weekend for you."

"No, I should have been with you."

She nodded. "I could have used some moral support a few times."

He stood up and walked away from her to the windows, pulling back the draperies to let in the dim light of the murky afternoon. From where she sat, she could see the misty humps of the Rocky Mountains towering in the distance. Water dripped from the eaves of the building and droplets ran down the panes of glass.

"Where did you go from Las Vegas if you didn't come home?" she asked, suddenly curious.

He turned back to face her. "The first flight I could get was to Denver, so I took it. It's just as well. I was able to take care of some business I'd been neglecting."

Carla had a condominium there, too, she thought. But she pushed that notion away.

"I didn't bother to turn the television on or I would

have seen all the reports. According to Nolan, that was all he saw for a couple of days.''

"It's about to drive my family crazy," she told him. "I don't suppose they've found Kevin yet?" She looked up at him as she asked the question.

Scott shook his head. "Not at noontime." He came back to stand in front of her. "When is your dad due back?"

"Is it still Tuesday?"

"Yes." He smiled at her uncertainty.

"He said they'd have the Cessna repaired by Wednesday. I guess he'll be home sometime tomorrow."

"Jere said you had some more trouble with the oil filters but that wasn't the reason you went down. How did you get it down without any more damage than that?"

"Kevin knew how to read instruments, but he became extremely worried when the oil gauge light came on. I convinced him we might have to force-land and, when he went back to fasten himself into the seat, I flicked the motor off and on a couple of times to make it seem that we'd lose power. When we dropped several hundred feet, he was sure it was more than oil pressure we were losing.''

"And then?" he prompted.

"Nothing. Luckily, the road was clear, and I told them we were going to land on it. Nobody got hysterical or anything."

"Tell me, Andy, what were you thinking when you knew you had to crash-land with seven passengers— one of them threatening your life and the lives of your passengers?"

Her eyes had been on her hands, clasped tightly together now in her lap. She looked up at him to see a glint of anger in his eyes.

Taking a deep breath, she exhaled and told him, "I was hoping Jere had sent in the payment for the insurance on the Cessna."

Chapter Twelve

Scott's lips moved but no sound came from them. He was standing in front of her, gazing down at the tumbled hair, the tanned face without a semblance of makeup. Andy's eyes were the color of the clouds lying atop the mountains, when they are misty with light rain. Her slim shoulders were bent slightly forward as though she was tired.

"Have you ever been spanked?" he asked suddenly.

She stiffened. "Not lately."

He sat beside her, one arm along the back of the couch, catching her chin with his other hand. "Then I won't break the tradition." He bent to place his mouth lightly on hers and, involuntarily, she gasped.

The instant thrill that swept her body parted her lips beneath his, and he took advantage of that to slip his tongue inside. But only for a second. His mouth left hers and she was pulled against him, both his arms around her, holding her close.

Catching her breath, she lay there, her mouth against the open throat of his shirt. She breathed in the smell of his after-shave and the cool dampness from the Windbreaker he was still wearing.

"When I left you Sunday morning, I wasn't sure whether to murder you in your sleep or stay and try to make you love me." His breathing was rough as he went on. "The plane you were on could have been hijacked and I'd never have known about it, I was so mad at you."

She tried to shake her head but was held too tightly to his chest. "I'm sorry, Scott," she whispered. "That's all I can say. I'm really sorry."

"You said that before. I was hoping you'd have a little more detail to give me if I caught you at the right time."

How could she tell him how she felt? The dislike of intimate relations that were painful....

Lying close to him, her hands aware of the hardness of the muscles along the back of his ribs, she tried to think. Scott was asking her this time. He was asking if he could make love to her without being rudely shoved away at the last moment.

I don't know the answer, she thought desperately. *What if I do the same thing again?* She closed her eyes, burrowing deeper into his shirt front.

"Scott." The merest whisper carrying his name forced its way past her lips. "I have to tell you." He held her without speaking, waiting. She moved back to look at him, blinking rapidly. "The reason I..." Swallowing hard, she started again. "The reason I—I didn't want you to...couldn't let you..."

His eyes were hidden as he looked down into her face, but his voice was quietly tender as he said, "You can say it to me, Andy. You can tell me anything. Go ahead.'' He shook her a little.

It calmed her. In a low voice, with only a slight quiver she told him. In halting words she tried to describe what she had fought years to forget. Her uncertainty, her constant guard against any feelings that might lead to a similar situation.

"Andy, sweetheart.'' And then he held her close for a long time.

Without her being aware of how it was accomplished, his hand was inside her robe, touching her bare flesh. Splinters of warmth spread from his fingers as he slid them tantalizingly along her thigh, stopping at the crease where it joined her hip. Scarcely breathing, she waited. His hand slipped over her rounded buttocks, lifting her.

Her head went back and she was looking up into his face, the dark lashes hiding his eyes. But hers were wide open, beseeching.

He let out a hard breath as he stood and picked her up, striding into her bedroom. Placing her on her tumbled bed, he sat beside her. The tie on her robe was loose, and he undid it and pushed it aside. He bent to place his mouth between the small breasts exposed to him. With tiny kisses, he moved down over the flatness of her stomach to her thighs.

The heavens opened to show pink-lined clouds, the warmth of a sandy beach. Roses spread their perfume where once icicles of strangeness had formed. Fragrant breezes wafted across her cheeks, fanning impulses his searching tongue hunted with abandon.

She was aware of trembling, aware of trying to push

him away, and always, aware of the tortured ecstasy he was arousing in her. Her hands on his head were pulled away and held gently by her sides until their fluttering quieted and she dug them into the sheets.

Her heartbeat ceased as he gently took her where she had never been; where books had never explained and pictures had never shown her what could happen. She was incapable of sound; she couldn't cry out to let him know what she was going through. She had no way to tell him not to stop; she couldn't say that if he didn't stop, she would never be the same.

The world went topsy-turvy in dreamy slow motion, and her body twisted with it. Her hips moved up and he met them with kisses that turned her body inside out. As the heavens split and crashed, Scott's arms caught her and held her tightly. He listened to her whispered words, held his hand over the thundering heartbeat as he cupped her breast and kissed the turgid nipple.

Long after her body grew quiet, she held on to him. Her arms were wrapped around him, jacket and all. The robe was pushed up beneath her and he straightened it. She moved against him, feeling the rock hardness of his body boring into her bare softness.

He didn't speak and for that she was thankful. All she knew was that she had lived twenty-eight years for this moment. She didn't want anything to intrude into it.

Knowing that he waited for her to speak, waited for her to get ready to acknowledge what happened, she kept her eyes squeezed shut. The tenseness eased from her as the minutes passed. His hand still clasped her breast; the hand beneath her head moved up and down on her cheek. The tips of his fingers found her parted lips and lingered where her uneven breath caressed them.

"I'd better move, Andy," he said, "And you'd better get dressed." His breath came unevenly. "We'd be smart to go out and have dinner."

Before she could deny that was what she wanted to do, he was standing by the bed, looking down at her. She lay on her back, staring back at him. Her eyes were no longer gray; they were black with the emotion still filling her senses beyond anything she had ever known. It blanked out everything else, leaving her with the knowledge that her body, hers alone until now, would never be the same. The feelings she had always thought more or less under her control were at the mercy of Scott's marauding kisses, his expertness at exploiting those feelings she couldn't explain.

Neither of them made a move to cover her. Scott's eyes went the length of her long body and back to her face. He smiled a little and, placing his hand flat on her belly, bent to kiss her mouth.

"Hurry," he whispered as he straightened and moved to the door, going through it without a backward glance.

Afraid of breaking the spell, she didn't want to move. Her body seemed to swim in the warmth of Scott's embrace. Swinging her legs over the side of the bed, she stood up, swaying as her legs threatened to buckle. The floor beneath her seemed to float as she went to the bathroom.

For some reason she didn't want to see what she

looked like at the moment. She turned the shower on and walked straight into it. Even the washcloth seemed to touch exposed nerves on her skin. She was tingling as she dried with a thick towel.

Still refusing to look at herself in the mirror, she went back to the closet to search for a dress. Scott had said they'd better go to dinner; instead, she thought hazily, they should lock the door and stay here forever. She shivered at the ecstatic memory the thought of staying with Scott evoked in her.

It was damp and chilly. She found the gray-and-yellow-plaid silk skirt, which was gathered and gave her long hips some shape, and matched it with a long-sleeved pale-gray blouse she had never worn. Her hair, for once, seemed to shine as she brushed the light-and-dark strands loosely away from her face, leaving half-bangs to flutter in wisps over her left eye.

Adding a tiny bit of shadow to her eyelids, Andy hesitated with the lipstick, then deftly stroked a light gloss over the lower lip only. Nothing was needed to help the light in her eyes; the glow still lingered from Scott's loving.

Scott was tall enough so that she could wear her gray low-heeled pumps. As she turned in front of the full-length mirror, she found herself hoping he would like her looks. She frowned, trying to remember the last time she had really thought about pleasing a man with the way she dressed. Chuck didn't seem to notice what she wore. Occasionally, he would give a wolf whistle if she appeared at the swimming pool in one of her more daring suits that was little more than strings, but not often.

Now that she had finished dressing, she hesitated about walking back to meet Scott. Lifting her head, she moved one foot resolutely in front of the other until she opened the bedroom door and walked into the big room where he was waiting.

He had drawn the draperies and was standing by the window, staring out into the deepening twilight of the early-fall day. Across the miles of fertile land separating the airfield from the city, lights were coming on. In the rain, which had started again, the brightness seemed to waver and shift.

She wet her lips as he looked her over. "Will I need a jacket?"

"If you have a raincoat, you'd better take it. I'm parked at the foot of the steps, but we may not be as lucky at the restaurant."

She took her raincoat from the hall closet and he held it for her to slip her arms into it. Without releasing her, he turned her around to face him.

"This is against my better judgment, Andy," he said softly.

"But you said..." She hesitated, wondering exactly what he had said.

"I said we'd better go out to eat and we had. So let's go."

Confused, totally unable to think of going to a restaurant, she let him lead her outside and help her into the car.

"The club at Terrence Hills is open," he said, pulling away from the building. She knew of the private club for residents of that restricted development. It was not her usual choice of eating places.

They arrived in fifteen minutes, an almost completely silent drive from her apartment. An attendant took the car to park it as they went into the restaurant. Another attendant took her coat and his jacket. Informal attire was the order of the day. Somehow she had pictured suits and ties. She relaxed a little.

When the hostess handed her a menu, her hand was shaking, and she tried to grasp the heavy parchment tightly enough to stop it. She looked up to meet Scott's bright-blue eyes, surprising a gaze she could swear was tenderness.

She straightened in the chair, looked at the menu, then raised her head to look straight at him.

"Scott," she said, and stopped abruptly. What was there for her to say? He knew what he had done to her. He knew she was at a loss at what to say or do about the feelings he had molded to fit the situation. Wetting her lips, she tried again, unaware that the entreaty in her eyes had changed their color from light-gray to a wood hue.

"Scott." Unable to go on, she bit into her lips and waited a moment before trying again. He watched her, smiling only a little.

She lifted her head and said evenly, "Am I forgiven?"

Surprise lit his eyes at the unexpected question, and he studied her intense features before answering. "Forgiven, Andy?" He spoke in a low voice and she leaned forward to hear him. "I'm the one who should ask forgiveness."

She stiffened. She didn't want him to apologize. Not for the unequaled pleasure he had given her; not for the feelings he brought to the surface that until now she had only glimpsed occasionally.

"No," she said, shaking her head. "No, Scott, I—"

The hostess appeared, and he gave their orders without asking what she wanted. He knew that neither of them cared at the moment.

When they were alone again, he, too, leaned forward. "I should have known what was wrong, Andy. I should have been able to figure out that you didn't know what belonging to someone meant. But I didn't stop to think." His look softened. "I won't make the same mistake again."

She didn't ask what he meant. Their dinner was served, and they ate, but she was intensely aware of Scott, and that was all. He paid the check and held her hand as they ran through the rain to the car the attendant had driven as close to the door as he could get.

In the car, his mouth came hard against hers for a moment, taking her breath, before he pushed her into the seat. "Fasten your seat belt, Andy," he said, turning his attention to driving on the slippery streets. She kept her eyes on the changing lights of passing cars, running her tongue across her mouth to feel the imprint left from Scott's kiss.

It seemed a much shorter drive back, and she stifled a disappointed sigh. He would leave her and go home again. Back to Carla, to whom he had once been engaged. Or to someone else who knew what it was like to belong to a man.

Warmth spread through her, stinging her cheeks, as she again felt Scott's mouth exploring her body for the first time, shocking her into submission at first, then arousing her with tantalizing desire beyond imagination.

He stopped the car, and from a distance she heard the hum of another motor. When the car moved forward again, she looked up. They had driven into a garage opened with an automatic opener, the motor she'd heard.

"It's my place, Andy," he said, as he opened the door and reached for her hand. She looked around as they went through one door and through another door facing an elevator.

As they went up in the elevator he held her hand. She looked up when it stopped. They were on the third floor. He smiled as she turned to meet his gaze, but he said nothing.

There was neither number nor name on the door where Scott stopped and placed a key in the lock. He pushed the door inward, tugging gently on her hand to pull her inside.

He stood behind her as she looked around the plush suite of rooms. The furnishings were two shades of gray; the carpet was dark pearl. Heavy draperies were wine velvet. It was the look of luxury, making her feel a trifle uneasy. She was used to comfort but not luxury such as this.

"Let me have your coat, Andy," Scott said at her shoulder.

She shrugged out of the coat, and as he went to a closet to hang it, she walked to the middle of the room. Coming up behind her, he took her handbag and placed it on an end table. As he straightened, he turned her into his arms.

"I've been talking to myself all evening, Andy, instead of to you. I should have been telling you how lovely you are. How much I enjoy being with you. How much it meant to me to hold you this afternoon."

She tried to pull away, turning her face from him so she wouldn't have to look at him.

"No," he said firmly. "Look at me, Andy."

His hand on her chin forced her to do just that, and she caught her breath at the look in his eyes. His gaze slowly locked with hers and he lowered his mouth until it closed over hers. As soon as her lips parted for him, his lips clasped tightly, loosening again to allow his tongue to thrust its way inside the receptive opening.

"Darling." His low voice sent vibrations through her. He left her mouth to let his kisses trail along her throat to her ear. His whispered words of desire were mere warm breaths that she moved closer so as to hear him better.

She wasn't sure if the soft moans she heard came from her throat or his. Her lips were against his ear, and she bit easily, then slipped her tongue into the grooves exposed to her. The barely heard entreaty came from Scott then, and she melted against him as his hand went beneath her blouse to fondle her breast.

"Wait, honey," he said, and she clung to him as he lifted her, carrying her easily into another room. The bed beneath her could have been rough planks, but she would never have known, so intrigued was she by what Scott was doing to her. She was never sure who undressed whom but that didn't matter. At last they lay wrapped in each other's arms, seeking the answer to the demands of their bodies.

She had often heard the adage about time standing still. Now she knew what it meant. Nothing moved: not time, not she, not Scott. For the first time in her life she felt the outline of a man's body against hers without misgiving. She wanted Scott as much as he wanted her. His kisses awoke a hunger she had never known existed, and only Scott could take away that hunger.

Murmuring her name, he moved on top of her, his long legs holding hers still beneath him. One hand moved over her ribs along the idention of her narrow waist, over the flare of her hip. When he came to her thigh, he slowed the progress of his hand, easing it to the inside of her leg.

"Andy," he said quietly.

"Yes, Scott." Her breath was short as she waited.

"I may hurt you." His arms tightened once more and his lips were against hers. "Do you understand?"

She lay still, knowing what he said was true. Knowing it was something she couldn't undo, once it was done. The love she had for Scott was enough to convince her.

Her hands left his shoulders to touch his face. One finger traced his lips, so close to hers. Stretching her legs, she shifted her hips.

She smiled. "No, Scott, you won't hurt me. Love me. Oh, Scott, I want you so much. I need—"

Her voice stopped abruptly as he kissed her, at the same time lifting her hips to meet the thrust of his body. Her outcry was muffled an instant until he raised his head to look down at her. Perspiration stood on her forehead, and her eyes were wide. But not with pain.

"Hello, darling," he whispered.

"I love you, Scott," she said. "Hold me."

For long moments, they lay that way until, slowly, he began to move. The movements foreign to her body came naturally as he coaxed her, as he turned her to meet his demands—demands he tempered with gentleness.

Her breath came in short gusts against his throat, her fingers dug into his back. All at once, she stiffened and went still beneath him.

"Don't, darling. Don't stop now," he entreated.

"Scott?" Her emotion-packed voice was almost nonexistent; he almost didn't hear her.

But he lifted his head to gaze at her, seeing the blazing answer to his passion in her wide-open eyes. And he knew.

"Yes, sweetheart. Oh, yes," he said, kissing her mouth closed as their bodies met thrust for thrust, expanding and contracting rhythmically. Until he held the long, slender body in his arms, caressing the length of her, cuddling her the way she needed to be cuddled.

The woman who wasn't afraid to fly a plane or a helicopter; who had come through a hijacking worried about the man who had threatened her. The woman who, before now, had been afraid to let go to love a man because of one painful experience.

Scott loved her, not for himself but for her. He

gave her the knowledge that love can be the sweetest emotion existing if handled right; he gave himself to her before he took her for himself.

He pulled her close, his lips against her fragrant hair. "Andy, this is what you were meant for."

Tilting her head back on the pillow, she said, "Yes, I know." She smiled as she watched his mouth drift down toward hers.

Chapter Thirteen

Scott brought his robe for her, and Andy sat against
the pillows on his bed, waiting for him to come back
to her. Shyness tensed her body. Pulling the robe
more tightly around her, she huddled into its warmth.
She looked down at her hands clenched into the coverlet of Scott's big bed. It was a paler wine than the
drapes, with a gray geometric design in the center and
at each corner. Her fingers looked white against the
dark color.

The door to the bedroom opened, and Scott came
in carrying a tray with two steaming mugs on it. He
wore a white velour robe belted loosely around him.

Gray eyes lifted to meet brilliant blue. He didn't
smile as he placed the tray on the bedside table and sat
beside her. For a long moment, they gazed at each
other. His forefinger came up to touch the hollow of
her throat where the robe opened.

"How are you, darling?" he asked.

Fascinated by the sound of his deep voice calling
her darling, she wet her lips before she answered him.

"If I move, will I break?" she asked finally.

He was bending toward her as she spoke, but stopped to look straight into her eyes. He laughed, a deep chuckle that brought glinting lights into already-bright blue eyes.

"Andy," he murmured as his mouth barely touched hers. "Oh, Andy." His cheek against hers was slightly rough with the beard beginning to shadow it. He raised his head, and his curious forefinger traced her cheekbone to her straight nose, tapping it before he kissed the tip.

He shook his head. "No man will ever break you, Andy. You fly a plane; you do anything you want to do. Why would you be afraid of a mere man?"

"I'm not afraid, Scott. I just never knew... I never wanted to know what it was like to belong to..." There was bewilderment in the shake of her head.

She was staring into his face, seeing the tenderness there, the gentleness in the wide mouth that taught her so much. He turned away and reached for the mugs, handing her a cup.

"Hot chocolate," he said. "With marshmallows."

She remembered the brandy he made her drink in Las Vegas. This was different. He didn't have to quiet her hysteria this time. She sipped the hot liquid, watching him.

"Move over," he said, and she scooted over to sit cross-legged beside him. Propped on a pillow against the headboard, he faced her across his steaming cup of hot chocolate.

"What kind of schedule do you have for this week?" he asked.

"A flight to Jackson Hole on Thursday. I'll be there

overnight. Then Saturday is instruction day. I have a favorite student coming, a girl.'' She wondered what his reaction would be. ''Kim's thinking of transferring to Louisiana Tech for more intense flight instruction. I unpacked all my old books and tests to let her look them over.''

Conflicting expressions chased over Scott's face as he listened to her. A slight smile touched his mouth, but he didn't mention Kim.

''Aren't you ever afraid, Andy? I mean *really* afraid?'' He bent toward her.

''Yes, Scott,'' she said simply.

''But no one would ever know just by watching you.'' He was obsessed with the idea that she was never afraid.

''It isn't necessary for anyone to know, Scott. What would that accomplish?''

''When have you ever been afraid?'' he insisted.

She had finished her hot chocolate and looked down into the mug resting on her knee. *How about in your arms, Scott,* she wanted to ask. *How about being afraid you won't come back to me after you leave me tonight? How about... ?*

Laughing a little, she said, ''I can't count the times I've been afraid. Surely, the latest incident was when I looked around at Kevin and saw that gun. I've never seen anything so ugly.'' She turned the mug around, looking at the design on it. It was the same geometric figure as on the bedspread. ''The day with you and Mother when I lost oil pressure. Not a catastrophe in itself, but it could have led to big trouble.''

''How about at Monarch in the helicopter?''

"I hate fog." He reached for the mug, and she un-curled her fingers to give it to him. "It's like what I think being blind would be. You know there's some-thing out there, but you don't know what. You've been there a thousand times and you know the land inch by inch, but when the fog closes in you lose all sense of direction." She looked up at him. "Yes, I was scared."

"Come here," he said, holding his arms out to her.

Coming up on her knees, she twisted and sat down in the curve of his body. With a sigh, she placed her head on his chest, sliding her hand beneath his robe. The wiry hairs created an electric sensation she liked across her palm, and she continued to rub back and forth over his chest.

When he whispered her name, her body uncurled to move into the curve of him. One long leg went across his. He pushed her head back, searching for her lips. All the magic was back. He gathered her to him, murmuring quietly over her mouth, kissing behind her ear. Heightened feelings followed his touch, down her slim arms to clasp her fingers between his, bring-ing them back over his hip to feel the tenseness there. Then both his hands cupped her buttocks, grasping them to pull her against his hard body.

Looking down into her face, lashes spread over her thin cheeks, he asked, "Are you afraid, Andy?"

The lashes swept upward. "Yes," she whispered.

His lips, which had softened hers, tightened, and she felt his withdrawal.

"I'm afraid I'll wake up and none of this will have happened." She pressed upward into his body. "I'm afraid you're going to make me wait...."

His kiss was swift and hard, catching the breath she exhaled. His fingers caressed her thighs, and she tensed even as she arched her back in aching need.

"Honey?" And quickly they were together. He didn't hurry but kissed her, letting her tongue inside his mouth, where he gently wrapped it with his.

The sounds she heard came from her throat. She moaned, trying to get closer to him. He released her mouth and her long, drawn-out sigh relaxed her body, allowing him to get closer to her. The rhythm of his body's movements changed, and her own body adjusted as he clasped her fully into his arms.

Her fingers dug into his back and she gasped, her head twisting on the pillow. She bit into her lips. He was watching as her lips parted, heard her indrawn breath, saw the light in her eyes. He kissed hard, smothering her outcry.

Minutes later, her body stopped trembling. Reluctantly he withdrew from her, pulling her into his arms as he lay down beside her.

"CAN YOU STAY with me tonight, Andy?" the voice asked near her ear.

Drowsily, she moved closer to the body lying with her. Realization was slow in coming, and when it did, she put her head back on the pillow. Scott was propped on a pillow, her tousled head on his bare chest. His silvery hair was rumpled, a thick section lying across his forehead.

"I'd better go home. Jere will expect his coffee to be made in the morning."

Scott's thick brows—dark, laced with some of the

silver color of his hair—rose. "You mean you still have to make coffee? Liberation decrees you at least share that chore."

"Not at Air Service. Jere and Avery make the world's worst coffee. I do it in self-defense." She sat up to look down at him. The sheet slid from around her and her slender body was exposed from the waist up. Reaching for the cover to replace over her shoulder, her hand encountered Scott's.

He held her hand, dropping to place it on her thigh, holding it there. "Kiss me," he said.

Leaning over, she put her mouth over his, spreading tiny kisses across it, turning back to let her tongue flick along his lips. His hand on hers tightened to hold it, sliding along her thigh.

His breath came more quickly as she teased him. Her free hand went out to lay flat on his chest, curling into the mat of hair. She slid her hand downward to the hard stomach where the edge of the sheet rested.

"Are you going to stay?" he whispered.

"I'd better not," she whispered back.

"Then I suggest you leave now...right now."

"All right," she agreed. She slid across his body, pressing into him as she did so. He reached for her, but she stood by the bed, laughing down at him as he smiled up at her. The smiles and laughter disappeared as they gazed at each other.

He touched her leg, and she turned to find her clothes.

THEIR GOODBYE KISS was brief when he finally stood just inside her doorway. He was holding on to her arms and didn't let her body lean on his as she wanted to.

"I'll let you stay here alone only if I don't get too close to you, Andy. In which case..." He let the sentence drop, kissed her hard on the mouth, and opened the door to leave. "I won't be able to see you tomorrow but I'll call you tomorrow night if I get back early enough." He opened the door and looked at her standing where he left her, her fingers holding the kiss he gave her. "Call me before you leave Thursday, anyway, will you?"

"Yes, Scott. Good night." She wondered where he would be the next day but refrained from asking.

In bed, she lay quiet, her body a thing of curiosity to her. It now belonged to Scott, not to her alone. It was an odd feeling. Sleep came as she smiled, remembering.

"SURE AM GLAD you're back to make coffee, Andy," Jere said. "The weather's beginning to demand it instead of lemonade, don't you think?"

Andy came from the storage room wiping her hands on a paper towel. "All you have to do to make good coffee, Jere, is to read directions. How many times do you have to remember that one big scoop makes four cups?"

He shook his head. "I never did learn metric figures. Maybe that's why I was never as good a pilot as you." He pointed to the cartons she had opened. "How do the oil filters look?"

"Aside from their being extra thin, I can't find anything wrong. Is it possible we had two flukes out of all those?''

''I don't care if they are flukes, they go back. Don't use any more and change the ones you have in the planes. Next time you might not be so lucky.''

That was the way she spent the day. Checking oil lines and filters. By three o'clock, she was filthy and everything smelled and tasted af oil. Even her coffee.

She had showered and changed into a red knit pantsuit when she heard the Cessna coming in. The sound of the motor was as familiar as her heartbeat; she'd recognize it anywhere. She ran down the steps to wait for Avery and Lawrence.

''Sound as ever, Andy,'' Avery told her as she questioned him.

''No oil gauge problem?''

He shook his head. ''No problems at all.'' He was leaning against the counter. ''There's been no sign of Kevin Engle, either. It turned real cold that night after a rainstorm, and the searchers say that unless he knows how to take care of himself, he could freeze.''

She winced. Kevin didn't deserve that, no matter what.

''Oh, yeah, Andy,'' Jere said, turning to look at her. ''Remember Scott's girl friend, Carla?''

She stiffened. Carla had been forgotten in the past twenty-four hours. She was back in the picture with Jere's casual question.

''Yes, I remember,'' she said, trying to keep the choking sensation out of her voice.

''She and Nolan Walters flew in this morning.

They'll probably need a flight out over the weekend if you'd care to fly the elite group back to Great Falls."

With a stifling pressure in her chest, she remembered how Scott told her he couldn't see her today. "Call me before you leave Thursday," he had told her. Just call him. Don't try to see me, I'll be tied up with Carla, he might have told her.

No, Scott, don't break my heart just yet. Fool around with someone else's heart, not mine. Perhaps he wasn't after your heart, Andy, a small voice reminded her. He wanted to see how afraid you really were of being a woman.

Ice water flung into her face wouldn't have gotten her attention more quickly. *No,* she thought. *It wasn't like that. Scott felt more than just curiosity; he had to feel something like I did to make me love him.... Oh, Lord!*

"What day?" she asked, as though it made a difference.

"Late on Saturday or Sunday morning. They'll have some more of the seed. Must have impressed someone."

"Sure, Jere. I have nothing better to do. Sign me up."

"You got a date with Chuck on Saturday night?"

Chuck. She'd forgotten all about Chuck.

"I haven't seen him since his fishing expedition. I'm not sure he'll be in town this weekend."

The phone rang, and she stood listening to Lawrence and Avery discussing the parts needed for the repairs and how to add that information to the insurance report. She wandered over to the door and looked across the field toward the Rocky Mountains.

It was still misty, but weather reports were optimistic that it would clear tonight and temperatures would be in the high sixties the next day.

"What time is the charter tomorrow, Jere?" she asked as he hung up the telephone.

"Eight-thirty."

Good. It was late enough that Scott should be up and around to talk to her before she left. She hoped he'd be alone. Her fingers bit into her arm and she looked down at the dull red impression they left in her flesh.

He will, she assured herself. *He wants to talk to me as much as I need to hear from him.*

"How many are going?"

"Seven," he said. "A full load. They also said you might have some people coming back. They've been on a white-water trip and weren't sure if they'd make it back in time."

"Good" was her only comment. A load of passengers meant not too much time to think of anything else. But a two-hour trip wasn't all that long—if you have pleasant thoughts.

Declining Avery's dinner invitation, she called her mother to chat a minute, then started upstairs to the big, empty apartment.

The side door behind Jere opened, and she glanced around to see who would be coming in from the parking area at this time of evening. Carla and Nolan Walters breezed in as though they owned the place.

Andy's eyes went to Jere, seeing his easy grin at the two people who went to the counter. Carla leaned intimately across the narrow separation and put her hand on his arm.

"We're at loose ends and thought you and Fay would like to go to dinner with us," she cooed at him.

You ought to wash her mind out with soap, Jere, she wanted to warn him. *She isn't interested in Fay going— just you.*

"You, too, Andy," Nolan said. "We just talked to Scott, and he won't be back until real late tonight and said not to wait for him."

Where is he, Andy wanted to ask. How far away that he can't get back until late?

Before she gave a negative answer, which was tempting, she waited to see what her brother was going to do.

"I'd have to call Fay to ask her," Jere said easily. "What time you going?"

"We'll meet you at the club at Terrence Hills if you want us to. That'll give us time for a couple of drinks before you get there," Carla said. "If Fay can't make it, you can just drive over with us."

Aha! Andy thought, *the plot thickens. Fay will be available, don't you worry. Or else Jere won't go.*

Carla certainly did like attention from all available men. Especially those who belong to other girls. She wondered what Nolan Walters's interest was in this quintet.

She could decline, Andy thought. She certainly didn't want to be a fifth wheel. And maybe, just maybe, Scott would get a chance to call later.

"What about it, Andy?" Nolan asked, turning to give her a big smile.

Returning his smile with what she hoped was some

semblance of friendliness, Andy was about to decline when Jere hung up the phone.

He shook his head somewhat regretfully, Andy decided. "Fay has a bad cold and said she couldn't taste anything."

"Well, you still have to eat," Carla said, smiling directly into his eyes. Her fingers tapped gently on the back of Jere's hand and Andy was tempted to swat her hand away like a pesky fly.

She turned aside. Jere was old enough to look out for himself, she hoped.

"Would you like to go with us, Andy? We could meet them over there in about an hour." Jere was looking at her.

Her first inclination was to go ahead with her refusal, but they were paying customers, after all. She could put herself out to be a little more friendly.

She nodded, and Carla smiled as she turned to Nolan. "We'll be waiting for you."

When they had gone, she reached over and tapped Jere's hand and smiled her sexiest smile into his eyes. "'You have to eat, dahling,'" she whispered huskily. "Really, Jere, she's about as subtle as a Russian MIG at twelve o'clock high."

He grinned. "Public relations, Andy."

"*Public* relations are not the kind Carla's interested in, baby brother, believe me."

"Ah, come on, Andy. Why are you so suspicious? They're just being friendly."

She shrugged. "Whatever, Jere. Let's go eat. I'm hungry." The red pantsuit would do for dining, she hoped, since she had no intention of changing clothes

again. She and Scott had been casually dressed when—
Glory, she thought, shivering.

Inside the Terrence Hills Club, she glanced around.
It looked different from the night before. But last
night, everything had been colored by what Scott's
lovemaking had done to her. She had neither seen nor
tasted. Not food, anyway. She had tasted of the love
Scott gave her, and feasted on his kisses, had held an
abundance of Scott's embraces.

She inhaled sharply as she looked over the diners.
Carla and Nolan spotted them from across the room
and waved, and Jere held her arm as they followed the
tuxedoed waiter to go to them.

"How long will Scott be gone?" Jere asked when
their orders had been taken.

Carla looked first at Nolan, seated across from her,
then at Andy. "It's hard to say. He never knows how
long the checkup will take."

Andy was instantly all attention as Jere followed up
with, "What kind of checkup?"

"Oh, he has some kind of injury from the military
service and it bothers him sometimes."

"We don't really know what happened," Nolan
said. "Scott never talks about it. Only he was shot
down over Vietnam and was a prisoner for a while. He
has nightmares about it yet and is still not very fond of
flying."

A flash of insight set her thoughts spinning. "Aren't
you ever afraid, Andy?" he had asked her several
times. No wonder he questioned her about being
afraid.

"But he—" she started to say when Nolan interrupted her.

"He's been going on short trips lately, and they don't seem to bother him as they used to." Nolan grinned. Andy thought again she didn't quite like him, even if he was Scott's friend.

Oh, Scott, she thought. *Darling, darling.*

At the moment, she would have given anything to be holding him. She felt the hurt and the uneasiness in him, trying to realize what it must have been like to be shot out of the sky and held prisoner. She relived for a moment the instant she turned to look into the muzzle of Kevin's gun.

Carla was leaning forward. "But we're really celebrating tonight." She smiled as all eyes focused on her. "Scott called me to tell me he was getting over his phobia about flying." Her flashing eyes settled on Andy. "He's also agreed to give me his half of our ranch now that we'll be married."

Chapter Fourteen

Andy froze. A thousand poison-tipped arrows penetrated her body. A lightning shock wouldn't have immobilized her any more than Carla's statement.

Jere turned to Carla. "Hey, that's great. Has the date been set?"

Andy's eyes were on Carla. At least, she thought, she'll leave Jere alone and Fay doesn't have to worry about her anymore.

The conversation went on around her, and she made what she hoped were appropriate comments. The dinner was served in grand style, and somehow she managed to eat. But the sparkling wine was so sour in her mouth that it could have been vinegar.

The taste of Scott's kisses was replaced by the bitterness of realization. He had set out to find what made her tick. What made her afraid of being a woman. Why she seemed never to be afraid of anything but that one thing: being a woman.

Now that he knew she was no longer afraid, he could admit his own uneasiness about flying: a phobia left over from an unforgettable war, a real reason for fright. Hers was only waiting for the right man to teach her how wonderful it was to be a *real* woman.

This is what my reluctance was about, she thought, placing the shining knife along the edge of her plate. *Somehow I knew when I fell, I'd fall so far it would break me to pieces.*

Jere touched her arm and she jumped, looking blankly at him for a moment. "Carla wanted to know if you'd be back from your trip to take them to Great Falls."

She nodded. "I'd rather leave Sunday morning, not late Saturday afternoon," she said over the constriction in her throat. "If there's no one returning with me, I'll drop you off and come right back. I have some new students coming in for orientation on Monday."

Perhaps Chuck would go along with her on Sunday. He loved flying in the De Havilland Otter. She'd make sure that was available. It was the least she could do for a friend.

Sitting in the midst of the conversation around the table, she heard Carla's sultry laughter and watched the graceful movement of her hands as she talked.

Scott was her silent partner on the ranch, she was telling Jere, leaning toward him, her long fingers lying intimately on his arm. The desire to slap her hand away came back again, but Andy put her hands in her lap, clenching them together. Jere was comparatively safe from Carla if she was marrying Scott.

I wouldn't bet on it, she thought viciously, and went back to half-listening to the talk around her.

"What about the hijacking of your plane, Andy?" Nolan asked.

She picked up her water glass to sip from it, carefully replacing it in the same damp spot before she answered him. "What about it?"

"For goodness' sake, Andy," Carla said impatiently. "It was all over the news, everyone wondering about the man who did it and why. How you put the plane down on a road. Of course we're curious."

Of course you are, she thought, taking in the smooth perfection of the girl's skin; the amber eyes going over Andy as though wondering why anyone would care what happened in a small plane figuring in a hijacking. Why, everyone knew hijackings only happen to huge commercial airliners going to faraway places. And no one was even hurt in the "routine" crash landing. Nothing to really talk about.

"I don't know anything about Kevin Engle except he was a harpist with Wyatt Stern's symphony group. He was recommended by someone from Denver and is very talented. That's all. On private planes, no one is searched for weapons, so it was easy for him to carry them aboard."

"How exciting," Carla commented..

"Yes," she said dryly. "It's very exciting to take off on a routine flight home and turn around to face a gun aimed at your head. It also helps when you have to take a plane into unfamiliar territory without a flight plan. A state highway is *not* an ideal landing spot for a Cessna." She stopped, aware that with each word, anger was building within her.

Anger directed at herself. Her first flight out with Carla's group had warned her she was out of her element. The idea that she would probably never see any of them again, Scott included, had made her careless. Her protective armor where men were concerned had slipped, exposing her to a fatal injury. She couldn't even file a claim with Blue Cross.

"If it had been me," Jere was saying, "I'd have been so airsick, the hijacker would have had to land the plane. *That* would have been a real switch." He gave his sister an affectionate glance. "Not to mention being scared to death."

"You weren't afraid?" Nolan asked.

"Aren't you ever afraid?" The question ricocheted through her head.

"I was afraid," she admitted quietly. What in the world is wrong with people who think if you don't go to pieces, you aren't afraid?

Carla shuddered delicately. "How could you land a plane with a gun pointed at your head?"

"I had very little choice," she pointed out, trying desperately to keep her voice polite.

The waiter interrupted at that moment, and she blessed him for it. The conversation switched to other topics and away from her. She sat motionless until they made a move to leave.

Although her body remained still, her thoughts refused to lie dormant. The voices around her were only so much noise as she let her mind rerun her night with Scott. When it had finished its destructive circle, she took a deep breath, rising to follow the others from the dining room.

She must have said good night because she found herself sitting beside Jere, driving back toward the airfield.

"Satisfied now?" he asked.

"Did I miss something you said?" she asked, in turn.

"You were worried about Carla having designs on your kid brother, right?" At her nod, he went on, "Well, now, you don't have to worry, since she and Scott will soon be married. You were looking for a fight where there was nothing to fight."

The blow to her chest took her breath for a moment before she answered him. "Yeah, but I wasn't watching for that left hook."

"What does that mean?" he asked.

He had stopped by the stairs leading up to her apartment, and she looked up at the darkened windows before she answered him. "That's the first thing you watch for in a fight, isn't it? The unexpected left hook?"

"I guess."

"I got the idea somewhere that she and Scott were an ex-item. The announcement that they'd marry took me by surprise, that's all."

"Does it matter to you?"

Her head swiveled at the tone of his voice. Jere had seen more than he let on. But when? Everything had happened in the space of just a few days. Scott had only lodged himself inside her heart to her knowledge on Saturday night. Last night, he cemented himself there with a perfection she hadn't thought possible. Her inattentive attitude at the club must have sent Jere a hint.

She opened the car door, turning to slide out. "No, it doesn't matter to me. It amazes me the way some people change their minds with the mountain breezes."

"Change. That's what makes the world go round, Andy," he said. He leaned down to see her as she stood outside the car. "See you tomorrow."

Lifting her hand as he drove away, she made her way slowly up the steps. The damp chill penetrated her jacket and she pulled it tighter around her to shut out the wind.

Inside the big room she stood in the darkness a long time, unwilling to see where Scott had been. Where he had gently questioned her. Where he had...

She made an impatient sound and flipped on the light switch. She was not the first woman to come to the conclusion that she'd waited half a lifetime to make a fool of herself over a man. She doubted she'd be the last. But tomorrow was a workday. She couldn't afford to lose sleep over him.

Easier said than done, she concluded, as she lay wide-eyed hours later. She had gone over every word of conversation between her and Scott. Not only every word, but every kiss and caress he had given her. She had found nothing that remotely resembled a commitment from Scott. He had set out to find what made Andy Timmons a good pilot and less of a woman.

The only promise he'd made was to call her "if he could." Instead, he had called Carla to tell her how well he was doing in his fight against fear of flying. And you can also have all the ranch in your name, he must have told her in so many words.

Her thoughts went to Kevin. What was he afraid

of? She sighed. I guess we all try, one way or another, to get rid of our personal phobias. I think I'll go back to mine; it's easier on the system.

LAWRENCE STOOD with her, looking at the Cessna 421 that had been repaired. Insurance people had checked it out, and it was ready for duty again.

"You think you should take the De Havilland, Andy?"

"Why?" When she thought Chuck would go with her, she had planned to take the De Havilland. But Chuck wasn't available, and she liked the Cessna.

He shook his head and grinned. "Well, with your luck in this one lately, I thought..." He let the sentence drop.

"The third time's a charm, right? This trip should be the one that makes my fortune. Maybe for the return trip I can pick up a wealthy client who will make us rich."

"Doesn't hurt to dream," he said. "Just thought I'd mention it in passing."

Laughing, she turned away to see Avery striding toward them. He put his hand on Andy's shoulder, smiling at her. "Meant to tell you that Boyce called us over the weekend. The baby you went into Monarch after? The mother has been released and the baby's fine. They'll keep it in the hospital a few weeks until it gains more weight."

"See, Lawrence?" she gibed. "I do get some good news occasionally."

But not always, she thought as she watched the group of passengers settle down and fasten themselves into the seats. Shaking her head, she concentrated on the controls, on the voice telling her wind velocity and direction, and followed the instructions to taxi to runway 21.

The wind wasn't strong enough to matter and she lifted from the runway into a smooth takeoff, her glance first sweeping the horizon, then below her at the tawny golds and browns of the trees. Some of the leaves were already falling, a sure sign winter was on the way.

Ski buffs were her stock in trade when the ski areas opened on slopes in northern New Mexico, Idaho, Wyoming and Montana. Staying over at the resorts sometimes, she was able to observe the techniques of skiing. Being an unskilled manipulator of skis, she even took lessons when the instructors weren't too busy. It was fun being on skis. Like flying a plane on the ground. At least, when you tumble, you don't have far to fall.

Turning her attention to the line of mountains on her left, just north of the Continental Divide, she headed west by northwest. The day was clear; no weather problems. Flying over the ribbon of Highway 187 out of Rock Springs, she headed into the small airfield at Jackson, Wyoming.

Three other planes sat near the hangars as she taxied smoothly to the slot, following the signalman. Smiling her goodbyes to the departing passengers, she got out to meet Osborne, a mechanic she knew from previous visits.

"I'll be here overnight," she told him. "We'll go over it tomorrow morning if you have time then."

"That's good, Andy. I'm kinda busy right now with everybody coming in for the weekend. We're expecting our first big snow tonight."

Until then she hadn't noticed the low ridge of light gray clouds lying over the towering peaks of the Grand Tetons.

"A little early, isn't it?"

"Yeah. We have plenty of the man-packed stuff and the weatherman first said it would be midweek before the snow came. They just moved it up a couple of hours ago. You know how these weathermen are. They guess a lot."

Casting another uneasy glance at the sky, Andy went inside the ready room to file her manifest and place a call to Jere.

"I got here all right," she told him. "According to the listings, the group that wants to catch my return flight won't be in until early tomorrow morning."

"That's what you expected, wasn't it?"

"Yes, but I wasn't expecting a weather forecast of heavy snow tonight."

"What? We have nothing indicating that, not even the long range forecast they sent us." Jere's voice was disbelieving.

She laughed. "I know, Jere. Look on the bright side. The forecasters could have their usual luck and be wrong."

"I hope so. Oh, by the way, Scott called early this morning. You were just lifting off."

Swallowing over the fullness in her chest, she asked, "Is he worried about the flight to Great Falls?"

Jere hesitated a moment. "He seemed concerned about you. He left his number for you to call him. Got a pencil?"

"Yes." As he read the number, she wrote it down, staring at the figures as they appeared on the paper. She was familiar with the Terrence Hills exchange. The number she was looking at was not in that area.

Probably Carla's hotel room, she thought, her mouth tightening. She crumpled the paper and stuck it into her pocket.

"He said it was important, Andy," Jere was saying.

"Sure, Jere, I'll call him to see what kind of problem he has."

If he was over his fear of flying enough that he can charter a small plane such as hers again, after recent happenings, he must be doing all right. Her sympathy returned as she recalled that an unpopular war had been the cause of his problem. If he had been receiving treatment for an injury, he was recuperating now after all these years, according to Carla.

Her fingers curled around the piece of paper in her pocket but she turned away from the telephone and caught a ride into the city. Luckily, there were rooms available in the motel where she had stayed before, and she signed for overnight.

Outside again, walking down the boardwalk, she stopped occasionally to look into store windows. The usual tourist items were there among Western wear jackets of insulated material popular in the skiing areas.

Her walk through the small town didn't take long, and she turned back to the motel. She wasn't ready for lunch but she was tired. The restless hours of the night before were beginning to catch up with her.

As she lay across the bed, she faced the telephone and lay staring at the instrument a long time. Finally, she raised herself up enough to read instructions on how to call long distance. Her jacket lay at the foot of the bed, and she reached inside the pocket to remove the wrinkled paper that had Scott's telephone number. She picked up the receiver and asked for the number, calling collect, identifying herself to the operator.

The receiver at the far end was picked up and she heard a voice, not Scott's, answer. The sound came through clearly.

"This is Nolan Walters. Mr. Rawlins isn't here at the moment. May I take a message?"

She hesitated, almost able to see the sardonic gleam in Nolan's eyes as he spoke. "Yes, operator, would you leave word for Mr. Rawlins to call me at this number?"

Why was Scott worried about her? Perhaps not. Maybe Jere just thought he sounded worried. Did he want to tell her about his coming marriage before anyone else had a chance to enlighten her? Too late, Scott. The bomb fell early.

She turned on her back to stare at the ceiling. A moment later she rolled over on her stomach. That was no better. She got up and went to the window and pulled open the draperies.

The clouds no longer lay over the Grand Tetons. They had settled over the tops of the mountains surrounding the city of Jackson. The afternoon looked all gray. Leaves gusted down the sidewalk and people hurried now, pulling coat collars up around their necks.

Turning back into the room, she pushed the button on the television set and flipped channels until she found one giving weather for surrounding areas. The high-pressure area had shifted, decreasing the chance of snow but dropping the temperature rapidly.

Breathing easier, she turned off the set. *Give someone else the snow for right now; let me get back home before you blanket this area,* she was thinking.

Time passed, and she grew hungry. She looked at her watch. Four o'clock and almost dark outside. Scott must be out for the day. At four-thirty, she went to the motel dining room to eat and was back in the room by five. There was no call.

Her mind refused to stay away from the night spent in Scott's arms. Her body refused to forget it. Scott, for whatever reason, had led her through the sweetness of belonging, of knowing the feelings that come with the love of a lifetime. Surrendering to her once-in-a-lifetime love.

"Nonsense," she scoffed out loud at herself. "Time will take care of your sense of belonging to Scott. Especially when he belongs to Carla for good."

She studied the navigation aids she always carried and halfheartedly read a paperback. At ten, she watched the local news and weather, assured of no snow before Sunday. She'd be home before the bad weather hit.

Scott didn't call. She hadn't actually expected him to. In bed, she did her usual twisting and turning before she slept a restless, tiring sleep.

"THE GUIDE with the group that was going back called, Andy," Osborne told her as he went over the plane with her. "They decided to stay a few more days since the snow was postponed." He laughed. "By the time they get back, we'll have that intermediate slope packed with good skiing snow and they'll stay another week." He shook his head. "Must be nice to have so much money you can't decide which resort to spend it in."

"Must be," she agreed. Carla. Scott. Nolan. Not Andy with her twenty-year-old Luscombe Silvaire and her faithful Cessna 421.

No complaints, however, she admitted to herself. She had always been happy with her lot. Her parents were neither rich nor poor. She had never suffered any trauma, nor had she ever done without anything she really wanted. Until now. She wanted Scott Rawlins with a raw, earthy desire she didn't know existed until he showed her. She loved him with a deep, soul-stirring passion she had read about, thinking at the time that the writer certainly knew how to use descriptive terms.

Wondering why he had called Jere to say it was important he talk to her and then did not return her call, she looked once more at the sky. It was cold and windy, but the clouds had all but vanished over the southern ridge of the mountains.

Scott Rawlins was doing what he wanted to do—

playing with her feelings. If she were smart, she'd admit that to herself and stop thinking about the hours in his arms. Hours she was sure would never be duplicated between the two of them. And, for her, never again.

In the control room, she drew her flight plan, checked the weather forecast once more, and waved goodbye to the airfield crew members. At nine in the morning, on a cold, windy day in mid-October, she lifted the Cessna into the wind and headed south.

Chapter Fifteen

That was that. Scott stood outside the hospital, looking around. Everything stood out in bold clarity. The film that had obscured his vision for so long disappeared with the doctor's final evaluation. He was a free man, free of uncertainty.

His phobia about flying was under control; he walked without a noticeable limp. His next checkup was a year from today.

And he was in love with Andy Timmons.

His release from the hospital so early in the morning was a surprise, and he couldn't wait to get to a phone. He sighed regretfully as Jere told him Andy was just airborne.

"Do you think she'll call in, Jere?"

"I'm sure she will, Scott."

"Ask her to call me collect, will you?" With Jere's assurance that he'd relay the message, all he could do was wait. Impatiently. He went to work to catch up on some of the backload he'd neglected while he chased Andy around the sky.

He grinned to himself. It was well worth the chase.

I can't wait to hold her again, he thought, feeling the tightening of his body as he recalled Andy's surrender to him.

Tenderness mingled with desire for her. What it must have cost her to tell him she was afraid of being loved!

"Oh, Andy," he whispered, closing his eyes tightly.

He was still waiting for Andy's call late that evening when Nolan came into his office. "Did you take any calls for me today, Nolan?"

He sensed a hesitation and looked hard at the other man. "Well, Carla called, but she said it wasn't important since she'd see you tomorrow."

Carla was right. Whatever she wanted could wait until tomorrow. He was interested only in Andy's call. He mumbled an answer to Nolan as he left, and went back to thinking about Andy.

As SHE TOPPED twenty thousand feet, rising high over the Grand Tetons, Andy looked down. Snow was packed with glistening brightness in the higher elevations. Firs and evergreens grew in thick acres on mountainsides. Over the ski resort nestled miles from Jackson, the wisps of smoke from lodge chimneys drifted like silver threads in the thin air.

Giving a check of the instruments, a long look at the oil pressure gauge and her fuel, she found her flight pattern and sat back to enjoy the smooth ride. Jere would much rather she brought back a load of paying customers, but she'd rather be up there alone.

Grinning to herself, she hummed a line from the operatic theme Wyatt's symphony members had played that fateful Saturday night. Her lighthearted thoughts wavered, remembering the desperate lines around Kevin's mouth as he pointed the gun at her. Why? He hadn't harmed them, hadn't done more than insist that she take him to Vancouver. Not Vancouver, Washington, but in British Columbia.

Frowning, she tried to figure where he might have gone from Pendleton, Oregon, back into those uninhabited mountains. There was absolutely nothing there. Still, no one had seen or heard from him. Not even the forest rangers who patrolled every foot of the forest and flatlands in the area.

Alpine was below her, then Stewart Mountain. She followed the stream below across the Salt River Range. Bridger-Teton National Forest was east of her. As soon as she broke free of the Commissary Ridge, she could head straight due east and drop down between the Medicine Bow Mountains and Park Range. From there, it was only a hop and skip above the Arapaho National Forest over Rocky Mountain State Park—and home.

Unfastening her seat belt to stretch and flex her legs before she refastened it, she settled down for a routine flight.

The heavier pulling of the twin engines was the first inkling she had. Her ears picked up the faint vibration, only a breath of difference—but she felt it. A quick glance at the controls showed her everything was normal. She turned her head to look at the wing on her left side. It was icing. So was the right one.

"This will never do," she said aloud, promptly dropping to sixteen thousand feet. It didn't help. She went to fifteen thousand feet, reluctant to drop lower because of the high ranges.

As the minutes passed, she knew she had no choice. This was one of the rare times when the lower air was colder than in the higher elevations, and the ice became thicker. She could chance trying to climb over twenty thousand feet with the heavy ice pulling on her or she could drop more. Or she could try to make it back to Jackson. Better not.

Making her choice, she dropped to twelve thousand feet, slowing her speed as she did so. Below her, thick forests carpeted the mountainsides. Not much of an opening if she had to go down.

Drawing in a shaky breath, she muttered, "Look, Jere, I was just kidding. I really don't care to make your life any more exciting. This is ridiculous."

Would Scott still be afraid if he were here? Would he relive the crash of his plane as he was shot from the sky? She'd probably never know. Even if she came out of this all right, he and Carla would be married... She swallowed hard. She didn't want him to marry Carla; she wanted him for herself.

In Las Vegas, Scott had laughed at her. But somehow, it hadn't been an insulting laugh. At the time, it hurt. Then he'd held her without forcing her to submit to his lovemaking. He couldn't know how much she had wanted to.

And then he came to her after the hijacking. Her breath sucked into her stomach, tightening it. It was hard to believe he had decided to marry Carla just after that.

He plays with everyone's heart, she decided, her

worried eyes on the layer of ice thickening on her wings. *This is what I've waited all my life for. Scott taught me that I'm a woman who can love and be loved. I want him to stay with me.*

Play with someone else's heart, Scott, not mine. Keep mine just for you.

Shaking her head as much at the thought of Scott as she did at the ice on the wings of the plane, she dropped another two hundred feet, looking straight down into the thickness of the trees. It was beginning to snow.

When the vibrations began, she knew she was going down. There was no way she could go up, and the ice was becoming too heavy for her to keep flying.

Flipping her radio for instrument ground clearance, she spoke into the mike. "This is CT6426NA to ground control. Do you read me?"

There wasn't a chance, and she knew it. She was too far down between the ranges. Turning the dial to the international emergency frequency, she gave the Mayday call over and over as she felt the plane dropping rapidly.

Drifting down her airspeed, she aimed for what looked like a clearing. With the gear down and flaps lowered to a minimum, she let the plane settle, slowing her speed, and felt it stall. Her best bet was to keep the nose up as much as possible, until she got to that thick grove of spruce firs.

Seven seconds after that thought, the plane hit.

SCOTT'S MIND remained on Andy as the hours passed. Wonder filled him as he recalled the raging desire that followed her reluctant confession. It was so easy to be gentle with her. He sucked in his breath, looking at his watch for the hundredth time.

Unable to stand the wait any longer, he placed a call to the motel in Jackson where Jere had said Andy stayed. A calm voice told him that Miss Timmons had left more than an hour ago. His call to the airport near Jackson confirmed that she had filed her flight plan and was on her way to Longmont.

He went to breakfast at the club, dawdling over it a lot more than he usually would. The flight from Jackson took about two hours if the weather was good—and the forecast was for clear and cold weather, fine for flying.

It was almost ten when he arrived at the private airfield administration building for Air Service. As he entered through the side door, Jere was standing behind the counter, telephone in hand, an anguished look on his face. His free hand rubbed over his chin and his eyes were closed as he listened.

"Yes, all right," he said slowly. "Yes, we'll stand by."

As he hung up the phone, he saw Scott standing there. "That was voice communications out of Montpelier, Utah. They picked up a Mayday signal from Andy's plane going down in the Salt River Range."

They stared at each other. Jere's face was absolutely white. Everything inside of Scott crumbled as he heard again the staccato sound of ground fire and felt his plane disintegrate as he slammed to earth.

JOLTED FORWARD over the controls, Andy heard the crashing sounds as though from a great distance. The groans and creaks of the heavy metal plane echoed in the stillness as the wind swayed it in the treetops. Half-lying in the seat, she let her eyes go over the inside of the cockpit. The windshield was intact. No glass sprayed over her.

Struggling upright, she crawled uphill to the door, pulling herself up to look outside the plane. Tops of some smaller trees were sheared off, but she had landed in a thick grove of evergreens, cushioning the plane.

Good thing she still had her rabbit's foot, she thought, biting on her tongue as she struggled upward. The plane rocked, vibrating with a loud crack.

Reaching the window, she saw snow coming down. She tried to see what shape the plane was in. It was tilted at too much of an angle for her to see from her vantage point. She crawled along the slanted floor and got back into the passenger area. Two seats were pulled loose and had tumbled against the side tilted downward.

From the inside, she couldn't tell what damage had been done. It really didn't matter at the moment. She was lodged inside, which was as good a place to be as any with the snow thickening by the minute.

Making her way back toward the cockpit, she fumbled with the radio controls. Her hands were beginning to go numb from the cold. Static was all she got from the frequencies she tried. She punched the send button and sent a distress call anyway. Someone somewhere might pick it up.

She sat in the crooked cockpit seat and took stock. It was cold, but she was unhurt. From what she could tell, it would take a bit more than a day to repair the Cessna this time.

If someone had heard her broadcast, they would start a search. Finding her in the dense area of the Salt River Range might prove to be a matter of guessing the right direction.

She pulled a blanket from beneath the seat and wrapped it around herself. Her feet were beginning to go numb and her fingers hurt from the cold. The weathermen had guessed wrong again. Or perhaps the cold front had reversed itself, as it had a tendency to do this time of year, following the line of least resistance over the mountains. It ended up in the southernmost tips rather than in the higher Rockies, simply because it was easier.

Just like people, she thought, huddling deeper into the blanket. As she got warmer, she grew sleepy. Realizing the danger in that, she stirred and sat up.

I certainly have tried my family's nerves in the past month, she thought. *Avery may ground me forever if this keeps up.*

Her eyes fastened on the window above her. It was already thickly crusted with snow. She knew she should try to get that door open, but it was too warm where she was and she didn't want to get outside in the icy wind. The cracking of tree limbs as the snow became heavy and the wind snapped them off testified to the fact that the temperature was plummeting rapidly.

Dozing fitfully, she stirred, trying to keep awake. She knew how people froze to death; it was so easy to sleep.

Noisy banging woke her. "Anyone in there?" a muffled voice called. "Hallo-oo."

Go away, she was thinking, *I'm tired.*

But the ruckus continued, and she struggled from what must have been a dream. She was in Scott's arms, warm and comfortable. Pushing the blanket away, she stared around her. There was only dull gray inside the plane. Snow had covered windshield and windows, insulating her from the wind.

"Hallo-oo?" The call was below her now, and the banging shook the cabin of the plane.

It took a moment before her voice worked. "Hallo-oo," she answered back.

The noise ceased, then resumed, as whoever was outside began prying on the door above her. The scraping noise was ice and snow being removed from around the door. She couldn't help. The plane sat at such an angle that any way she tried to go was uphill—except the window she half-lay against near the cockpit.

A long time later, the muffled voice called, "Are you all right in there?"

"Yes."

"Can you push against the door from the inside? The pressure from the ice and snow is holding it down, but if you can help..." The voice was caught by the wind, and she missed the last part.

Making herself push away the blanket, shivering in protest as the icy air hit her body, Andy pushed herself upward. She was stiff and was sure she'd never be able to reach far enough over her head to help.

I'd better, she told herself. *Whoever it is may get disgusted with me and leave me here.*

It seemed hours before she braced against the metal frame of the door. "I-I'm here," she called, her voice cracking with the cold. "What do you w-want me to d-do?"

"Can you get any kind of hold on something so you can push upward?"

Her feet were numb. Looking down at them, she realized she was wearing cowboy boots, not her usual sneakers. She had given in to the colder weather.

"W-wait a second," she called, her breath an icy stream in front of her.

Sliding her long body alongside the door frame until she was stretched at an angle, she brought her legs up until her boots caught beneath the molding.

"Okay. I have my feet against the door near the handle."

There was silence and, for a moment, she panicked. Had he given up and left her? *I'm trying,* she wanted to call out.

"Right, Andy. Now, when I give the word, shove as hard as you can."

Andy? The voice was unfamiliar, but he knew her name. Someone had heard her emergency call. Hallelujah! *I didn't think there was a chance.*

"Now!"

Braced against the tilted floor, she straightened her legs, straining against the weight above her. For a moment, nothing, then it slowly lifted.

"Keep pushing," the voice said.

She could see him working, placing a broken limb from one of the trees in the opening to hold the door back. His face was covered in a ski mask and he wore a knit cap.

"Can you stand up?"

"I think so." Letting her legs slide downward along the door, she pushed herself to a sitting position. A hand encased in heavy gloves reached for her, and she managed to hold on as he pulled her through.

Clinging to the burly figure, she looked down. Her plane sat some thirty feet off the ground in the top of broken and splintered trees. With a shuddering breath, she buried her face in the cold jacket beneath her cheek.

"Hang on, Andy. Just hang on to me. I'll get us down."

She was good at hanging on. Even her numb fingers cooperated as she clung to the bundled clothing of the man holding her.

It seemed hours before her fingers were gently disengaged and she was set on her feet. He still held her. "Can you stand up at all?"

"Yes, I th-think so." Her feet were almost numb, and her hands didn't obey her impulses. Snow blew into her face, and it was hard to keep her eyes open. She tried, gazing into the masked face she still didn't recognize.

They were away from the plane and he half-carried her over the snow. At a sled, made from small tree limbs, he pushed her down, wrapping another blanket around her. He left her, and she saw he was pulling the sled with a rope he had fastened around his chest, under his arms. Dreamily, she watched the bulky figure walk slowly over the fluffy snow. When he stopped, she was half asleep.

Looking around, she saw a log cabin. Smoke came from the chimney. She didn't know people were allowed to live in here, but she was glad this man did.

The man came back to lift her, carrying her easily into the cabin. He put her down near the brightly burning fire and bent to remove her boots. As he put them aside, he rubbed her feet hard.

"Are you hurt anywhere, Andy?" he asked.

"No. How do you know who I am?"

For a moment he didn't answer, busy taking off her heavy socks and massaging her cold feet. Taking a towel from somewhere, he wrapped her feet and turned them toward the fire. Then he reached up, removing the knit cap and the ski mask.

Her rescuer was Kevin Engle.

Chapter Sixteen

"The chopper's here, sir," the young man in bright-blue coveralls told Scott. "Here's a printout of weather conditions in the Salt River Range area."

"Thanks." Giving the printout a brief look, he watched the Jet Ranger helicopter set down a hundred yards away. Regarded as the Cadillac of helicopters, it was heavy-duty, just what he needed where he was going.

There had been no further word on Andy's plane, but he hadn't stayed around the airfield very long. As soon as Jere cleared him, Lawrence flew him to Pocatello, not far from the small Idaho town that had caught Andy's radio signals.

Eyeing the noisy helicopter, he had a moment's trepidation at the thought of getting at the controls. The machine looked like a monstrous insect as it sat awkwardly waiting for him. The apprehension lifted as he stepped aboard, followed by an off-duty forest ranger, Dick Abrams, who had volunteered to go with him.

Touching the controls lightly, he realized he hadn't

forgotten a thing about flying a helicopter. The ones he was familiar with were not like this one. The army hadn't progressed quite that far. The grin that touched his mouth was almost a grimace, when he remembered some of the equipment they had used to fight a war. He turned his attention to getting the Jet Ranger into the air.

Over Montpelier he reached ground control, checking to see if any further word had come from Andy. Rangers were searching but they hadn't found her yet. The snow was thicker, the temperature dropping.

"I was stationed on the range a couple of years ago. Go in at the southern indention here." Dick Abrams pointed to the map he held. "You can see some trails to follow up part of the way." He shifted his finger a half inch. "And here, there's an old abandoned ranger cabin. There should be enough space by it to set us down. We can ground-search from there. If the plane went through the trees, it'll be hard to spot."

Scott nodded, following the area Dick traced with his finger from the highway through secondary roads to hiking trails over the higher elevations.

They ran into the snow as he turned north, leaving the guidelines of the paved highway behind. Wind blew the snow across the windshield of the helicopter. If it started to stick and freeze, they could have a problem.

There was little time to think about flying again. Then Dick said abruptly, "Isn't that smoke I see?"

He hovered, dropping down to get a better look at where Dick was pointing. It could be a wisp of cloud that low, but it could also be smoke.

"What do you think?" he asked.

"I think it's smoke. If you can clear that low range to the east of us and come in on the other side..."

Lifting a hundred feet higher, he went in low over the range Dick had indicated and came around the end of it. Below them, in a small clearing, was a cabin. Smoke came from the chimney, swirling around with the snow until it was almost invisible. Dick had good eyes to have spotted it.

"Any sign of a plane?" Scott held his breath.

"No. It's probably a hunter decided to hole up in the cabin till the storm passed. Think it caught a lot of people by surprise, since it was supposed to have gone way north of us."

Grimly Scott remembered the optimistic weather forecast. The same one Andy had listened to, he was sure.

Taking a deep breath, he dropped his speed, sinking rapidly toward the cabin, feeling the push of the wind against the helicopter. A blast took them unexpectedly, swinging them around. It took a moment to steady the machine and drop into the open space by the cabin.

"Go ahead and see who's there," he yelled to Dick. "I'll be ready to take off as soon as you get back."

As Dick swung from the helicopter, the door to the cabin opened and a tall man emerged. He walked to meet Dick, and Scott saw him nod, white teeth flashing through a thick beard as he grinned.

When they motioned to him to cut the engines, Scott was out of the helicopter and running toward the cabin almost before they could lower their arms.

"She's here; she's safe!" Dick said.

He stood there immobile, looking from Dick to the stranger who had come from the cabin. Snow blew into his face, stinging with its fierceness. Without a word, he walked past them and pushed the door open.

Andy lay on the floor in front of a roaring fire. Wrapped in blankets with only her head showing, she was asleep. The noise from the helicopter hadn't been enough over the wind to wake her.

Kneeling, he looked down at Andy's serene face. Her lips were chapped, skin peeling a little from windburn or frost—he couldn't tell. Her dirty blond hair had never been more beautiful; sweeping lashes were several shades darker as they lay on her tanned cheeks. Her mouth was too wide to be pretty, but it held a sensuous shape that caused his world to spin crazily.

A shaking finger went out to touch her as he heard the two men come in behind him. She stirred, and her eyes opened slowly, focusing with difficulty in the firelight.

Amazement widened her eyes, showing the translucent gray rims surrounding a dilated pupil. "Where did you come from?" she asked incredulously.

"I couldn't resist the chance to show off," he said, bending to kiss her.

Pushing the blankets away from her, he gently extracted her from their warmth, pulling her to him. She was wrapped in another lightweight blanket, evidently nude beneath it. Without looking at her, he tucked the covers more closely around her as he held her close in his arms. His lips moved over her face as his hands patted her shoulders. Murmuring softly into her hair, he gradually became aware of the other two men standing nearby.

He looked up and for the first time got a good look at the man with the beard. He stiffened. "Aren't you—?"

The man nodded. "Yes, I'm Kevin Engle. Believe me when I say it's good to see you again."

Scott looked down at the woman in his arms. Still wide-eyed with disbelief, she stared back at him.

"How did you find us so quickly?" she asked.

"Quickly?" He groaned. "It took us forever." He looked around, spotting a bench by the fireplace. He lifted her and went to sit on it, holding her in his lap.

"Isn't it still Saturday?" Turning her head, she tried to see out the small, snow-covered window.

"Yes. It's getting dark, though. We won't get out of here tonight."

"The storm's getting worse," Kevin told them.

Scott looked down at her. "I could worry about that if I weren't so damned glad to see you without a scratch." He squeezed her. "That brother of yours is right."

"How so?"

"He said you were a good pilot."

"Wait till he sees the Cessna." She bit her lip. "I wasn't as lucky as when we went down with Kevin."

"I don't care if it's completely unsalvageable as long as you're all right. Are you? Really?"

"My feet are a little frostbitten and my fingers are still numb. Otherwise, I'm fine."

"I don't suppose you have some kind of radio

rigged up to get word to the outside world?" he asked, turning to Kevin.

Kevin shook his head. "I haven't heard anything except what I picked up a few days ago in Montpelier." At Scott's questioning look, he smiled. "I went in to get some canned foods to go with the meat I caught. I heard they're still looking for me."

"It was a dumb stunt to pull," Scott said.

He looked down at Andy as she put her hand on his chin to turn his face toward her. "Carla and Nolan told me you had to go for checkups, that you were hurt while you were flying."

He nodded, waiting.

"She also said you were planning to marry soon." It was going to hurt, but she had to hear him say it. "She said you were giving her the ranch because you'd be married and..." Her voice drifted away.

"I told her we'd settled the ranch question. I also told her I planned to be married."

She squinted over the tightness in her chest, turning her head away so she wouldn't have to look at him.

"Not to her, Andy. I'm not getting married to her."

"It doesn't matter who you're marrying," she said stiffly. "It's none of my business, of course."

"Of course," he agreed quietly.

Swallowing with difficulty, she started over. "I didn't know you were uneasy about flying. Why didn't you tell me?"

He laughed, looking down into her face. His eyes brightened as he kissed her mouth lightly. "Tell Miss

I'm-not-afraid-of-nothing-nor-nobody that I was scared to death to fly? Not on your life.'' He pulled her back under his chin, rocking back and forth on the bench with her.

He could tell her later whom he was marrying, she guessed, lying close to him, loving the strength of his arms. She moved back to look at him.

"What I was going to say is that Kevin had a lot of problems stemming from the war, too. His aren't as easily defined as being afraid of something specific like flying, or...or...''

"Or having someone love you completely?'' he finished for her. The tenderness in his voice brought a stinging to her throat, and she bit again into her sore lips.

They had forgotten the two men with them. Kevin had put an old iron kettle on some of the coals in the fireplace and now he poured boiling water into old cracked mugs.

"I decided that even if they did pick me up, I had to have coffee,'' he was saying as he mixed instant coffee for all of them. Dick accepted a cup, looked at the two people on the bench, and passed it to Scott.

"Sit here,'' Scott instructed Andy, placing her beside him.

She leaned against him. What would she do when they got home and he married someone else? She was almost too tired to care and, for the moment, he was holding her. He had braved a vicious winter storm and his own misgivings to come after her.

"Now, then,'' Scott was saying, "do you suppose we can start somewhere near the beginning and make some sense out of the entire story?'' He held the mug of coffee to her mouth and waited as she sipped it. ''First thing, why didn't you return my call while you were in Jackson?''

''I did. I gave Nolan my number at the motel.''

''When?'' His eyes narrowed as he waited for her to think about dates and times.

''Friday evening about six, I guess. Somewhere near that, anyway. He said you were out and I asked that you return my call. You didn't.'' Her voice turned slightly accusing. ''The least you could do is call me and tell me yourself that you were planning to marry soon. Especially after... after...''

He didn't say anything, but she could feel him looking at her. After a long moment, while her body tensed beside him, she raised her head to meet his look.

''After what?'' he asked.

''After you... after we...'' Unable to continue, she shook her head. It had been hours since she thought of the feelings Scott had aroused in her. Now they were back. With his breath on her cheek, she could also feel the warm rivulets of passion he sent flashing through her newly awakened senses. She quivered.

Avoiding his steady gaze, she looked at Kevin and Dick. They sat talking quietly on the opposite side of the fireplace. Scott bent to put his mouth close to her ear.

''After we made love? After we set off our own rocket launch? Is that what you're asking, Andy?''

''Yes.'' It was a whispered answer, but it was enough for him to hear.

"I don't know why Nolan decided to lie about it, but I asked if you'd called. He said no."

She frowned. "Why would he do that?"

"It doesn't matter right now. Perhaps he thought I'd draw all the money out of Carla's ranch since I'd found out how much you mean to me. He thought, possibly, you might be jealous of my leaving money in the ranch."

Wide gray eyes looked directly into brilliant blue ones, shuttered now by the dark lashes contrasting strangely with his silvery hair. Her mouth opened, but no sound came out. She shook her head.

"You mean you don't know I love you? That I, along with all I own, belong to you?"

His voice was teasing, but the blue eyes darkened as he waited for her answer.

"When did—did you...?" She stammered, trying to get the words past a suddenly stricken tongue.

"I don't know, darling. Maybe when I first found Andy Timmons wasn't a man but an upstart of a female pilot."

His arms encircled her, pressing her, blanket and all, against his chest. As she sat still, one hand moved around her to slide beneath the wrapping, touching the small breast with the tips of his fingers.

"Look at me, Andy," he said.

When she tilted her head back to look up at him, he was smiling, his mouth very close to hers. "I love you." As her eyes darkened, he asked, "Does that straighten things out in your mind?"

Looking away from him, her eyes met Kevin's. For a moment she remembered the haunting fear in those eyes and the reason for it. Turning to Scott, she said, "Yes."

"Yes, it helps, or yes, you love me, or both?"

"Both. Everything. It helps. I love you."

He laughed down into her face before he said, "I always love explicit answers to my questions. Especially when they're the answers I want to hear."

The hand resting over her breast beneath the blanket slid down over her hip, lifting her body back into his lap. He rocked back and forth, his lips resting on her hair.

"I was hoping for a happy ending to this trip, but I really wasn't expecting this," Dick said, grinning at them as they sat as close as they could get.

"There's going to be another happy ending," she said, and put one hand up to rub Scott's cheek.

"What's that?"

She looked up then. "Kevin will need help to get back into the veterans' hospital and get out of the hijacking charge."

Scott's eyebrows were climbing and questions were in his eyes. "Yes?"

"I'll drop all charges against him if you'll use your influence to get him back into the hospital. He left without permission, and they're hard-nosed about taking patients back after that."

"They should be," Scott said, glancing across at Kevin, who sat quietly listening to the exchange.

Turning his face back so he had to look at her, she said, "I know, but there are extenuating circumstances." Her eyes simply asked for understanding. "You will, won't you?"

"What makes you think I can help?"

"Can you?"

The love in her eyes was plain. For a moment he was tempted to accuse her of coercement, but instead he smiled. "Probably," he said as his mouth covered hers. The kiss was brief, but he still held her close as he turned to Kevin. "Maybe I could think of a way to help if I knew more about your circumstances."

Kevin nodded and began to talk in a tight voice. "I was against the Vietnam war, but I fought anyway. Everyone in my outfit knew I hated it; I was bitter." He stared into the fire. "They sent back every one of my buddies blown apart, or just the dog tags. I hated twice as much the many people that kept the war going. It was wrong. They killed our men, innocent civilians; they tore up the country. And Washington gave us their pat answers to the world's problems and ignored it all. The worst part is we'll do the same thing somewhere else in the world."

"Why were you in the hospital after all that time? A bad injury?" Scott's voice was quietly interested. His predicament after the war hadn't been so different from Kevin's. He was lucky to have outstandingly knowledgeable and sympathetic doctors.

"Not physically. I couldn't forget how many were hurt, though."

"Where's your family?"

Kevin smiled a little. "I don't have anyone. That's why I joined the symphony group; it was Wyatt's family. And I'm a good musician, too. It's all that kept me going."

"You never forgot your music in all those years?" Andy asked.

"We had a musicians' group at several of the hospitals I was in. I kept in practice. It was good therapy."

They talked into the night. Pots of coffee and meat roasted on the open fire satisfied their hunger.

Hours later, they lay wrapped in blankets, Andy cradled in Scott's arms. Outside, snow fell silently, but inside it was warm.

Kevin would get the help he needed and deserved. She was no longer afraid of sharing her love with Scott. And Scott... She sighed as his arms tightened around her.

Scott sat near her, leaning forward, half-turned to look at her as he talked with Avery. Her mother listened to their conversation, keeping her eyes on Andy most of the time. It had been a trying weekend for them all.

After Scott flew her out of the mountains in the Jet Ranger helicopter, he put her in the hospital emergency room in Montpelier and went back for Kevin and Dick Abrams. Her parents flew up and stayed overnight on Sunday, flying them all back to Longmont on Monday.

Aside from sore feet and tender hands, she bore no ill marks from her crash. It would be several days before they could go in after the Cessna.

"What about Kevin?" Avery asked.

Scott sent a glance at her before he answered. His voice was quiet as he talked about the incident.

"He was wrong, of course, but desperation does strange things to people." Again he looked at Andy; this time, he winked. "I've been there." He stood up and walked away from her, turning around as he went on. "I know people who can give us some pointers on the best way to handle his case. We'll take it from there. Is that all right with you, Andy?"

She looked up quickly. "Of course, Scott. Why are you asking me?"

"Because you were the one who was hijacked and who crash-landed. He also saved your life. You're going to figure pretty big in the decision."

"Oh." She sighed, quite tired of it all. "If it were left up to me, I'd forget the entire past several weeks. Wipe them out completely and start over. It's been a catastrophe from day one."

He came back to stand in front of her. "Really?" Reaching down, he pulled her rather roughly up into his arms. "And where would that leave me, Andy?"

They looked into each other's eyes, reliving the best parts of the past weeks. She leaned against him, putting her arms around him to hug him tightly.

"I guess you're right. In case the genie is listening, I retract that statement." Straightening away from him but not letting go completely, she said, "Thanks for the dinner, Mother, and for the pep talk, Avery. I should be able to make it through the week now."

Scott drove her to her apartment and unlocked the door to let her in ahead of him. Just inside the door, she stopped to let her gaze roam over the familiar surroundings. As Scott turned after closing the door, he slipped his arm around her, pulling her against his hip.

She leaned on him, conscious of the warm feeling inside at his touch. His fingers slid upward from her waist over her ribs, one by one. As he reached the slight swell of her breast, his hand stopped.

"Andy?"

Sliding her head back on his shoulder, she looked up, smiling. Scott wasn't smiling. The expression on his face was one of serious concentration.

"Come over here." He led her to the couch, releasing her arm as she sat down. For a moment, he stood looking down at her before he sat beside her.

"You're right. It has been a rather unsettling few weeks since we've met." He didn't touch her but leaned forward, one arm propped on his knee. His other hand covered hers, where it lay in her lap. "I guess as far as time is concerned, maybe we don't know that much about each other. There isn't much to tell about me."

"Why do you have white hair?" she asked abruptly, as he hesitated.

Surprise lit his eyes, then he laughed. "It turned white about the time I got shot down over Vietnam. That and a bad leg injury were the souvenirs I brought home. And I hated to fly after that. At one time I was like you. Couldn't get enough of airplanes." He took a deep breath. "For years I've ignored the fact that I was... well, yes, afraid to get back in a plane. Lately, I've gone back to flying and I'm getting better. Being around you helped that a lot."

Her hand went up to push back his heavy silver hair. "After you got over being mad at me for being a woman pilot?"

His look softened. "It wasn't that, Andy. Somehow I knew you were going to upset my very carefully set up dull way of life, and I already resented you for it."

Curious, she moved closer to him, lifting her face so that their lips were close. "How could you know that?"

"Because after I met you, I stayed angry all the time, wanting to bring you down to my level of being afraid of taking one of those beautiful planes into the air. I wanted you to feel as uneasy as I did."

She straightened up. "Then when you found out I was afraid of being a woman, it made you happier."

He shook his head. "The only reason I was happy about that was because I was the one you let change your mind about it." He caught her to him. "Oh, Andy, you were so precious to me there in Las Vegas. So scared, wanting me and not knowing how I ached for you."

"I thought you were mad enough to strangle me."

"I was." His lips moved over the wispy half-bangs across her forehead. "When Jere told me you had been hijacked, I felt the same terror as when I had nightmares about flying." He pushed her away to gaze into her face. Shaking his head, he said, "When I came here that night, nothing would have kept me from loving you. Nothing, Andy." Almost desperately, he caught her back to him, holding tightly. "That was the sweetest night of my life."

For a long time, they held on to each other.

"About Carla." She stiffened, trying to pull away, but he refused to loosen his arms. "About Carla," he repeated. "We were engaged years ago. After that, we were business partners. Her ranch was getting run down while she was busy doing other things. When she hired Nolan as her business manager, I consented to help them. Even lent her money for it, with half the ranch in my name."

"You don't have to explain all this to me," she said.

"I want to," he said simply. "I didn't give her my part, as she implied to you. She'll pay me back with the cattle she hopes to sell after the new grass they're trying produces more tender beef." He looked at her, smiling at the intense attention she was paying to his words. "I would have given her my part of the ranch except for you," he told her.

"What did I have to do with it?"

"In case you agreed to marry me, it's half yours. I can't give away what's yours."

Her eyes grew blank for an instant, then realization filled them. She wet her lips, but no words came.

"Will you?"

"Oh."

"That's all? Oh?" He waited, watching the play of expressions over her face, until the one he wanted settled there. A look of desire so total that he sucked in his breath.

"Scott." As she breathed his name, he caught her close. Her lips touched his ear. "Yes. Oh, yes, I'll marry you."

For a long time they sat motionless, letting their bodies adjust to the lessening of tension between them. When he finally pushed her away, he saw the tears on her eyelashes.

"Hey, you're not supposed to cry yet," he told her.

She sniffed. "I'm not crying."

"What do you call those?" he asked, touching the jewellike drops on her long lashes, watching them spread on the tip of his finger.

His wet fingertip slid down her cheek to her mouth and she tasted the salt from her own tears. The finger caressed across her lips, parting them, and went on around to her chin.

"It's getting late, and it's been a long day," Scott whispered. "I'll help you get ready for bed." He picked her up, his arms slipping easily under her long legs, slim and smooth in sheer panty hose.

She had dressed for dinner at her mother's, using clothes she kept there in one of the bedroom closets. Now, as he placed her on the bed, he kissed her cheek and quickly unbuttoned the red printed sheer silk dress, slipping it from her shoulders. As she lifted her hips for him to pull it down, her hands went up to hold on to him. He let her down easily, removing her underthings in one movement.

In a moment, he had pushed aside the covers. "Where are your pajamas?"

"I don't have any," she said.

He grinned down at her. "No?"

"There are some nightgowns in that drawer." She pointed to the heavy chest opposite the bed.

The grin faded from his face, but he continued to look down at her. Turning away from her soft look, he took a blue gown from the drawer and came back, handing it to her. Surprised, she watched him do an about-face and walk to the window. He didn't touch the drapes but stood with his back to her.

"Put the gown on, Andy," he said.

Doing as she was told, she said, "All right, it's on."

He came back to sit on the side of the bed. "I want to stay with you. In fact, I can't stand the thought of leaving you." He didn't touch her except with his eyes, but they were like torches going over her shoulders. Only a tiny strap held the gossamer material to her slender, tanned body.

"May I stay? I want to hold you more than anything in the world right now. There's always the chance you'll fly off into the wild blue yonder again, out of my arms, if I let you out of my sight for a minute." A tentative finger touched the thin strap over her left shoulder, pushing it aside to place his lips on her smooth flesh.

Her shiver was pure ecstasy.

"I promise to just hold you, Andy. You're so very precious to me."

She held out her arms. For a moment, their eyes held. When he lowered his face to hers, her hands were already busy with his shirt buttons. As their lips met, they both knew that holding wouldn't be enough tonight.

4 FREE
Harlequin Romances

TAKE THESE 4 Harlequin Romances FREE

Delight in **Mary Wibberley**'s warm romance, MAN OF POWER, the story of a girl whose life changes from drudgery to glamour overnight....Let THE WINDS OF WINTER by **Sandra Field** take you on a journey of love to Canada's beautiful Maritimes....Thrill to a cruise in the tropics—and a devastating love affair in the aftermath of a shipwreck—in **Rebecca Stratton**'s THE LEO MAN....Travel to the wilds of Kenya in a quest for love with the determined heroine in **Karen van der Zee**'s LOVE BEYOND REASON.

Harlequin Romances . . . 6 exciting novels published each month! Each month you will get to know interesting, appealing, true-to-life people . . . . You'll be swept to distant lands you've dreamed of visiting . . . intrigue, adventure, romance, and the destiny of many lives will thrill you through each Harlequin Romance novel.

Get all the latest books before they're sold out!

As a Harlequin subscriber you actually receive your personal copies of the latest Romances immediately after they come off the press, so you're sure of getting all 6 each month.

Cancel your subscription whenever you wish!

You don't have to buy any minimum number of books. Whenever you decide to stop your subscription just let us know and we'll cancel all further shipments.

EXPERIENCE
Harlequin Temptation ™

Sensuous...contemporary...compelling...reflecting today's love relationships! The passionate torment of a woman torn between two loves...the siren call of a career ...the magnetic advances of an impetuous employer–nothing is left unexplored in this romantic new series from Harlequin. You'll thrill to a candid new frankness as men and women seek to form lasting relationships in the face of temptations that threaten true love. *Don't miss a single one!* You can start new *Harlequin Temptation* coming to *your* home each month for just $1.75 per book–a saving of 20¢ off the suggested retail price of $1.95. Begin with your FREE copy of *First Impressions*. Mail the reply card today!

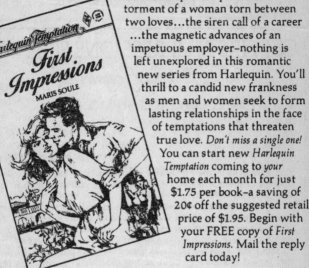

First Impressions
by Maris Soule

He was involved with her best friend! Tracy Dexter couldn't deny her attraction to her new boss. Mark Prescott looked more like a jet set playboy than a high school principal–and he acted like one, too. It wasn't right for Tracy to go out with him, not when her friend Rose had already staked a claim. It wasn't right, even though Mark's eyes were so persuasive, his kiss so probing and intense. Even though his hands scorched her body with a teasing, raging fire...and when he gently lowered her to the floor she couldn't find the words to say no.

A word of warning to our regular readers: While Harlequin books are always in good taste, you'll find more sensuous writing in new *Harlequin Temptation* than in other Harlequin romance series.
® ™Trademarks of Harlequin Enterprises Ltd.

Readers rave about Harlequin American Romance!

"...the best series of modern romances
I have read...great, exciting, stupendous,
wonderful."

—S.E.,* Coweta, Oklahoma

"...they are absolutely fantastic...going to be
a smash hit and hard to keep on the
bookshelves."

—P.D., Easton, Pennsylvania

"The American line is great. I've enjoyed
every one I've read so far."

—W.M.K., Lansing, Illinois

"...the best stories I have read in a long
time."

—R.H., Northport, New York

*Names available on request.